# HEARTLESS PRINCE

## AN ACCIDENTAL PREGNANCY ROMANCE

LILIAN MONROE

*Seize the moments of happiness, love and be loved! That is the only reality in the world, all else is folly.*

—Leo Tolstoy, War and Peace

1

————

# DAHLIA

I'M CURSED.

Always have been, always will be—but I've learned to live with it.

The barista doesn't know that, though. She just thinks the milk steamer on her espresso machine stopped working as soon as I walked up to the counter.

"Sorry." Her eyebrows arch. "It's never done this before." She glances at the door marked 'Staff Only' behind her, chewing her lip. I wonder if her manager is a hardass.

I shake my head. "It's fine. Forget about the lattes. I'll just have two black coffees."

"I'll refund you."

I smile. "Don't worry about it." I'm not going to punish her just because I'm perpetually unlucky.

Her shoulders relax a bit. She gives me a shy smile. "Okay —thanks."

I take the two coffees to the table where my aunt, Theresa, is waiting. She nods her chin toward the machine, which magically started working again for the next customer.

"What happened?"

1

"It's the curse."

Auntie T rolls her eyes. "Of course it is. You know there's no curse, right?"

"Try living a day in my shoes and then tell me there's no curse. This morning, I slipped on a banana peel in my kitchen. A banana peel! I don't even eat bananas! Unless this is live-action Mario Kart, that shouldn't happen to a regular person."

"Maybe you're just clumsy," she grins, "and isn't your roommate an athlete? Athletes eat bananas, don't they?"

I huff, sinking down into the chair across from her. The curse is real, and it sabotages me every day. Don't even ask me about my love life—that's in the Oxford English Dictionary under 'disaster'.

My roommate, Elle, would tell you otherwise—but she thinks just because I have a healthy sex life, it means I'm good at dating. I'm not. I've never had a relationship last more than a couple of weeks.

"How was the Prince's Ball, honey?" My aunt asks, bringing her coffee cup to her lips. With an oversized, leopard-print, faux-fur jacket and long crimson nails, she doesn't exactly look like she belongs in the campus café.

I can't meet her eye. I suck at lying—so, I just tell the truth. "I didn't go."

"What? But we received the thank you note from Farcliff Castle. They only send those out if you attend."

I scrunch my napkin between my fingers and take a deep breath. "My roommate went instead of me."

"Why would she do that?" Theresa's painted nails fly to her chest and her bright, red lips drop open. She frowns, as if Elle stole my invitation from me.

Elle didn't steal anything from me. I was the one who convinced her to take my place—and not very easily. She had no desire to go, but I'm glad she did. That's how she met Prince Charlie.

"I didn't want to go, Auntie T. You know how I feel about castles and crowds."

Theresa's eyebrow arches and she looks me up and down. "First of all, you know I don't like it when you call me Auntie. It ages me."

My lips tug into a small smile.

Theresa continues: "Second of all, why would you pass up the chance to go to the Prince's Ball? It only happens once every generation! Are you insane?"

"I didn't feel comfortable going up to the castle."

Theresa tuts, shaking her head. "I blame your mother for this. She scared you away from your own heritage. Why should a Raventhal daughter be afraid of meeting the royal family? It's all this talk about a stupid curse. No one should put those thoughts into a young child's head."

"She's right, though. It's not safe for me there."

Theresa pinches her lips and drums her fingernails on the table. She tilts her head, watching me. "If you're so scared of the castle, why—of all the places where you could study organic chemistry—did you choose Farcliff University?"

"Microbiology."

"What?"

"I study microbiology, not organic chemistry."

"I thought you said..."

"That was just one of my classes last semester."

She waves a dismissive hand. "Whatever. You're avoiding the question. Why come *here*? With your grades, you could have studied anywhere—yet you come to the one place that terrifies you." My aunt purses her lips. "It doesn't make sense for you to come here if you're just going to avoid the royal family. You live in a dumpy house on the edge of Grimdale, and you pretend your last name is Smith. You're a *Raventhal*, Dahlia. You belong up at the castle with the rest of them—so why avoid it?"

I take a sip of coffee and avoid her eyes again. She's right. I live near the edge of the poorer end of the Kingdom called Grimdale—hardly the typical neighborhood for a Raventhal to live. However, it's a perfectly acceptable place for a girl called Smith to live while she studies at Farcliff University.

Growing up, I was hidden away in the forests of the Rocky Mountains. I lived with my three aunts, who served as guardians while my parents lived in exile. I wasn't even told that I was originally from Farcliff until my sixteenth birthday. My parents would come and visit me twice a year, and my mother was the one who'd explained that I'd been cursed as a small baby.

That's why they took me away from Farcliff—to keep me safe from the curse. That's what my mother said, at least. My aunts would shake their heads and tell her to stop putting silly superstitions into my head.

I know how crazy it sounds, but that's the kind of thing that stays with you. Now, I'm supposed to be taking part in court life as if none of that ever happened? As if I haven't been told that going to the castle will kill me?

I sigh. "I don't know. I feel like an imposter. This is where I was born, but I was shipped away from Farcliff when I was a toddler. I never got to see the Raventhal home. Growing up with you, Aunt Helen, and Aunt Margie was..."

I trail off, lost in my own thoughts.

"It was what?" Theresa's voice has an edge to it.

I take a deep breath. "It was wonderful. I loved growing up in the wild. I loved being surrounded by nature and birds —even if being allergic to pollen, and bees, and insect bites isn't exactly convenient in the middle of the wilderness. Even so, it was peaceful. But... I don't know who I am, Theresa. All of a sudden, when I turned sixteen, you told me I was a Raventhal and that I belonged in the Farcliff Court. I just want..." I sigh, shrugging. "I don't know what I want."

I sip my coffee as Theresa studies me. When she doesn't say anything, I know she wants me to keep talking.

"Whenever I see Mom, she always tells me they're dangerous at court. And then you're telling me the opposite —pushing me towards it, telling me it's fine. Which is it? Is it safe, or not safe? Am I cursed, or not cursed?"

Theresa puts her hand over mine. Her face softens as she gently squeezes my fingers. "Your mother has her own ideas. I'm just trying to encourage you to be the Lady you were born to be. I want you to reach your full potential, Dahlia."

I take a deep breath. "I know Mom has always been paranoid about the Farcliff royal family. I don't want to live in fear like she does."

"So, why are you running away from it? Why not go up to the castle when you're invited?"

"It scares me. What happened with Mom..."

"What happened with your mother was unfortunate, but I don't know if it was really as bad as she thought. It was more of a scandal in the press than anything truly dangerous."

"You mean her exile?" I stare at my aunt and take a deep breath. "What exactly happened with her? All I know is that the Queen died, and Mom started claiming she'd been murdered—and then she was sent away. Whenever I ask her about it, she clams up."

Now, it's Theresa's turn to avoid my gaze. She stares out of the window at the stream of students walking toward their classes. "That's more or less what happened," she says.

"More or less? What does that mean?"

My aunt sighs. "It's not for me to tell, munchkin."

"Why not?"

"It was a long time ago, Dahlia. It doesn't matter anymore."

Frustration builds inside me until I feel like I'm going to explode. This happens every time I try to find out about the past. Whether I ask my aunts or my parents, I always get the same answer. It's in the past. I'm not old enough. It's not for them to tell.

Well, whose story *is* it to tell? How am I supposed to know who to trust in Farcliff if I don't know what happened, or why my mother was exiled? She used to be the Queen's best friend—now, I can't even ask anyone why that changed.

"The King's sister was spearheading the campaign to have your mother exiled," Theresa explains. She pinches her lips together and her lipstick creases. Her eyes tighten as she stares at me, and I hold my breath. No one has ever said anything about this to me before.

"The King's sister?"

"Lady Malerie." Theresa sighs. "She never liked your mother. I think Mal was insulted that the Queen asked your mother to be a bridesmaid and not her. Said she was the King's sister, and Tabitha Raventhal was a nobody. Very easily offended, that woman." Theresa tuts her lips and shakes her head. "Lots of drama surrounding her."

"I never heard about this."

"No," Theresa answers without explanation.

"So... Exiling Mom was payback? For not being asked to be a bridesmaid?"

"The bridesmaid thing started it all... And then there was Prince Charlie's christening. Phew! Don't get me started on *that*." Theresa shakes her head. "When Tabitha was named godmother instead of Lady Malerie? Well—all hell broke loose."

My heart thumps. No one has ever been this open with me before. I lean forward. "What happened at Charlie's christening?"

My question seems to snap Theresa out of her own thoughts. She looks at me, wide-eyed, and inhales sharply. She claps her hands together and shakes her head. "What are we doing, talking about things that don't matter? I'm here to take you out to lunch! We should be pampering ourselves, not talking about silly drama from the past."

"What if I want to talk about silly drama?"

"Well, that may be, but we have some self-care to attend to. Come on, I didn't come all the way from Colorado to visit my darling niece just to spend the whole time sitting in a cramped coffee shop. I've made us an appointment with Farcliff's best hairdresser. Your colors need some refreshing, and I need a blowout."

I run my hands through my multicolored strands and take a deep breath. I can tell by the look on Theresa's face that I won't be getting any more information out of her today.

Besides, my hair is dyed a rainbow of pastel colors, and Theresa is right—it does need a refresh. Sighing, I give in. She's told me something, at least. I can look into Lady Malerie, the King's sister. Maybe that will give me some clues as to where I come from, why my family was thrown out of Farcliff, and where this whole idea of a curse came from.

Aunt Theresa throws her arm around my shoulder and leads me out of the café just as my two other aunts, Helen and Margie, come screeching down the street in my orange Jeep. Helen has a bright blue headscarf on, paired with over-sized glasses, and Margie's long mane of silver hair whips wildly around her head. They whoop and holler toward us as everyone on the street turns to stare.

Theresa tugs me toward the Jeep and I let a smile slide

over my lips. My aunts taught me to live a loud, happy, colorful life. They were the best guardians I could have asked for—but I can't keep shying away from the questions that plague me. I can't keep living in fear of a curse that might not even exist.

I need to know where I come from, and what happened with my family all those years ago.

2

———

**DAMON**

MY BROTHER almost knocks my bedroom door down as he barges through it.

"I need your help." His eyebrows are drawn together and his forehead is creased. I've never seen him like this before.

I tuck my pencil behind my ear and turn away from my notes and textbooks. Studying can wait—Charlie's in trouble.

Charlie takes a deep breath. "Father thinks I'm dating Dahlia Raventhal."

"Dahlia Raventhal?" I frown. I didn't even know there was a Raventhal in Farcliff.

He nods. "Yeah."

"The daughter of Tabitha Raventhal?"

"Uh-huh."

"The woman who got thrown out of the Kingdom after Mom died?"

"Yeah, that one."

"And why does Father think you're dating her daughter?"

Charlie sighs, running his hand through his hair and making it stick up in all directions. He looks pale as he starts

9

pacing up and down my room. "Well," he starts, "I've sort of been dating her roommate."

I fold my hands in my lap. "Okay. Who's her roommate?"

Charlie grimaces. "You wouldn't know her."

"Try me."

"No, I mean you actually wouldn't know her. She's from Grimdale. She goes to Farcliff University on a scholarship."

"Ah." I pinch the bridge of my nose. Who Charlie dates is a big deal—he's the Crown Prince, after all, and he needs to declare a wife within the next few months in order to be named the official heir. So, of course, his wife needs to be someone 'suitable'.

Dahlia Raventhal is not suitable. Her mother was thrown out of Farcliff and disgraced after making wild accusations after the Queen—our mother—passed away. Marrying her would understandably cause some controversy.

But marrying a nobody from Grimdale?

Even worse.

Completely out of the question—to Father, at least. I doubt many other people in Farcliff would care.

I nod. "Okay. What do you need me to do?"

"Look, I just need you to pretend to be dating Dahlia. Father's spies saw me at Dahlia and Elle's house, and if he thinks I was only there because of you, it'll give me enough time to think of a solution."

It's a stretch. I don't know if my father will buy it. Charlie looks desperate, though, so I nod. "You really like this girl, huh?"

Charlie's lips pinch and he looks at me, eyes wide. His chin dips down. "Yeah. Yeah, I do."

I take a deep breath. "All right."

My brother releases breath and closes his eyes. "Thanks, man."

"What's Dahlia like? Will Father even believe I'm into her?"

Charlie's eyes flash and a tiny grin appears on his lips. "She's... unique."

"Unique-good? Or unique-bad?"

"Let's just go over there. I think it's better if we explain it together, and for you to actually meet Dahlia before she comes over for dinner."

THE DRIVE to Dahlia's house is tense. I've never seen Charlie so stressed. He won't stop pulling at his hair, and it looks like he hasn't had a decent night's sleep in days. His knee bounces up and down the whole way there.

I'd do anything for my brother. I don't like seeing him like this. Charlie is under a lot of pressure as the heir to the throne, and I know he doesn't want the Crown. None of us do —not him, or me, or our little brother Gabriel. But if Charlie steps aside, he's putting me on the throne instead. I'd much rather complete my studies at medical school and contribute something meaningful to the Kingdom. Maybe even the world.

Plus, I'm not cut out to be King. I know I'm not. I have too much darkness inside me for that—even if nobody else knows it except for me. There are too many demons warring in my own heart for me to live my life in service of the Kingdom.

It has to be Charlie.

I know he's taking the throne to protect Gabe and me, and I appreciate it.

So, if it means I'll have to pretend to be into some chick that happens to be one of the Kingdom's most recent enemies, so be it. That's fine. The only reason I'm able to pursue medical school in the first place is because I'm not the heir to the throne.

I owe that to Charlie. I know his relationship with our father is tense, so the least I can do is pretend to be into Dahlia.

I glance at Charlie, who's biting his lip and running his hand through his hair again. He looks stressed out of his mind.

Charlie said 'unique'. I like 'unique', I think. At least, I can pretend to like 'unique' for my brother.

When we get to the run-down house on the edge of the border between Grimdale and Farcliff, I bite my lip. This doesn't look like somewhere a future Queen or a member of court would live. Charlie jumps out of the car and strides toward the front door. I jog to catch up.

My eyebrows arch when the door opens and I meet his girlfriend, Elle. She's tall and athletic, with short brown hair. She's not at all the kind of girl I'd expect for him—but when I see his eyes soften and his lips curl into a smile, I know he's completely head-over-heels for her. He kisses Elle and a little twinge of jealousy courses through me.

My brother—the womanizer, the Kingdom's most notorious bad-boy, official playboy and heir to the throne—has somehow found a good woman to love, who also loves him back.

Me, on the other hand? Strait-laced, plays by the rules, unlucky number two?

Love doesn't even enter my vocabulary.

Not that I'd want it, anyway. There's too much rot inside me. I can't love anyone for the same reason I can't be King—I'm no good. I'm spoiled to the core. Unredeemable.

As Charlie whispers something to Elle, I try to stop myself

from heading down a spiral of self-loathing. I know where that ends up, and it's never pretty.

But I don't have to try too hard to stop my thoughts, because at that moment, Dahlia Raventhal turns the corner.

She's definitely unique-*good*.

She's also definitely completely, buck-ass naked. Not a stitch of clothing on her. My eyes widen and every drop of blood in my body floods between my legs. My mouth waters and my hands itch to reach out for her.

She's short, with small, perky tits that are begging for my touch. Her hair is a rainbow of pastel colors, and—Farcliff-fucking-Almighty—her pubes are dyed to match. I'd kill to watch myself pumping my shaft in and out of that rainbow.

She's a petite, fairy-like creature, and she looks like she'd be fucking insane in bed.

I aim to find out.

Charlie asked me to pretend to be dating this chick, but there's only one way to be truly convincing. I don't want to pretend at all.

Why should Charlie have all the fun?

It doesn't have to be love between Dahlia and me. I might have a black heart, but I can still enjoy a woman's company.

Dahlia glances at Charlie, Elle, and then me. She doesn't yelp or cover herself. She's not embarrassed to be seen without any clothing. She doesn't react like any other human being I've ever met.

No, the naked Dahlia Raventhal fucking *waves* at us. She flashes a smile and lifts her arm up, as if nothing at all was strange.

And I need her. Badly.

My body is burning up. My blood is sizzling through my veins. I can't think of anything except the rock-hard cock between my legs, aching to fuck that pixie princess.

I'm dizzy, barely able to stumble my way to the kitchen. When Dahlia reappears, she's wearing a sparkly purple robe and the only thought in my brain is that I want to see her naked body again.

Preferably on top of me. Or underneath. I'm not picky.

I could tangle my fingers into her multi-colored hair and claim those soft, pink lips. My mind flies in a thousand different directions, and every single one of them involves Dahlia Raventhal and me in various states of ecstasy.

Is she a screamer? What does my name sound like when she's moaning it into my pillows? What does that hair look like when it's twisted into my fist?

I can't take my eyes off her. She opens the refrigerator and grabs a fucking chicken leg, of all things, and watching her eat it is the most sensual thing I've ever seen.

She licks her fingers, and my mouth hangs open. I wish those were my fingers between those perfect pink lips of hers.

Charlie is talking, but I hardly hear a word.

Elle is freaking out, but Dahlia's eyes are on me and all I want to do is drag her back to the castle, lock her in the tallest tower, and fuck her into oblivion.

"Can we just back up for a second?" Elle stands up. "What the hell is going on?"

I can understand her reaction—this *is* a weird situation— but right now, I'm more than happy to help them out if it means I get to see Dahlia again.

"Look, it's no big deal," I interject. "My brother likes you, but he's the Crown Prince, so dating you is complicated. He needs a bit of time to figure out how to make that work. If our father thinks he's into Dahlia, it means you're safe. If our father thinks he's into *no one*, even better. I'm going to buy him some time by saying that *I'm* the one who's into Dahlia." I glance at Dahlia, and she smiles. "You two will be free to keep seeing each other without fear of retribution. Simple."

My heart is palpitating. Her smile sends a thrill straight through me, and all I want to do is tear that robe off her perfect body and plunge myself inside her.

Dahlia looks at Elle. "Seems simple to me." She shrugs and takes another bite out of the chicken leg.

The four of us come to a bit of an understanding. For a moment, Dahlia hesitates, but then she looks at Elle and I see her resolve strengthen.

I do my best to try not to look too excited at the prospect of seeing Dahlia again, but my eyes keep drifting over that sparkly purple robe of hers, picturing the body that I saw a few moments ago.

Charlie and Elle disappear down the hallway. Dahlia's eyes flick to mine and she sits down at the table next to me.

She intertwines her fingers, and I notice that her nails are painted with pink glitter. "We should probably come up with a back story," Dahlia says, tilting her head and studying my face.

"What did you have in mind?"

I love the way her lips tug upward, and how she twirls a sparkly pink finger around her teal, pink, and purple hair. I watch the movement, mesmerized. How would those pink fingernails look if her hand was wrapped around my cock?

"Well, maybe we could say we met at Farcliff University, or something?"

"I get private tutoring. Apparently, it's distracting to have royalty at college."

She chews her lip and the shoulder of her robe falls off. I catch a glimpse of her breast, sending another wave of heat through me. She tucks it back over her shoulder absent-mindedly.

Dahlia lets out a soft sigh and shrugs. "Maybe we met at a networking event, or something? At the Prince's Ball last month?"

"Were you there? I feel like I would remember you."

Her smile widens. "No, not me—but 'Dahlia Raventhal' was," she says, nodding down the hallway. I guess Elle went in Dahlia's place. That must be where Charlie met her.

I grin. "Okay, so we met at the ball and I dazzled you with my brilliance."

That makes Dahlia laugh, and I'm not sure if it's insulting or not. I don't really care. I want to make her laugh again.

"Right," she nods. "Maybe we met there, and we've been seeing each other a few times a week ever since. We study together, or something." She chews her lip as she thinks, her leg bouncing up and down. Her robe falls open again and my head starts to spin.

Does this girl not care that I've seen her naked multiple times, and I only met her fifteen minutes ago?

"Are you okay?" Dahlia puts her hand on my wrist, and heat zips through my arm.

"Yeah, why?"

"You look like you're about to pass out."

*Probably because all my blood is currently occupied some-where between my legs.*

"I'm good." I smile, and she pulls her hand away. I resist the urge to catch her fingers between mine.

Charlie reappears in the hallway way too soon. He nods to me. "We should go. Thanks for helping out, Dahlia."

"No worries." She smiles and gives us another wave before disappearing back into her room. Charlie drags me away and I throw one last, wistful glance at her door.

When we get outside, the sunlight hits me way too hard and I stumble forward.

"You all right, Damon?"

"I'm fine," I say, rubbing my eyes. "Totally fine."

Charlie is grinning at me. He shakes his head. "I'm guessing you're okay with this plan, then?"

"I mean, I'm a romantic at heart. I'll do anything for you and Elle."

"Uh huh."

We head back to the castle and I go straight to my room, lock the door and empty myself of everything Dahlia awoke in me.

# 3

# DAHLIA

RUSHING to scribble down the last of my notes, I slam my notebook shut and stuff it into my bag. Ever since Prince Damon's visit to my house yesterday, I've felt completely off-balance. I know it's just a dinner party at the castle, and I know that my aunts think I should try to integrate with court life a bit more, but it still makes me nervous.

I said yes for Elle, because I know she needs me. And maybe—in a small, forbidden part of my heart—I also said yes because I want to see Prince Damon again.

I sling my bag over my shoulder and hurry out of the auditorium. That was my last class today, but I need to rush to the library before all the good desks are taken. It's getting to midterm season, and everyone at Farcliff University is starting to freak out. At least studying will give me an excuse to not think about the dinner party.

The cold whips through my thin leggings as I make my way outside and across the Farcliff University campus. The science *building* is on the opposite end of the campus as the science *library*—which will never make sense to me. They should at least build an underground tunnel or something between them. It gets cold in Farcliff during the winter.

It's nearing the end of February now, and I can't wait for winter to be over. Farcliff is a small Kingdom nestled between Canada and the United States, to the east of Lake Ontario. The winters here are long and brutal.

My teeth are clacking by the time I make it across campus. I'm angling toward the door of the science library when something catches my eye.

No, not something—some*one*.

Prince Damon of Farcliff, to be exact. The very man that I've been trying to get out of my head for the past twenty-four hours.

He's leaning against a sleek, black car with his hands tucked into his pockets. When he sees me, he straightens up and lifts an arm.

"Dahlia!"

Heat zips through me and I forget how cold I am. How does he do that? Even yesterday, when he was in my kitchen, I could barely breathe.

It's just because he's royalty, I think. It's definitely not the way his forearms flex, or how his shoulders tug against the fabric of his top.

And right now, the heat zipping through me is just from the open science library door. It's definitely not Prince Damon's gaze.

I change my trajectory and walk toward the Prince. His face splits into a smile and his eyes drag all the way down to my faux-fur lined boots and then back up to my eyes. A current of electricity flows wherever his gaze lands.

"Hey." I try to sound casual as I walk up to him. My tongue feels too big for my mouth. Am I nervous? It must be the cold.

He nods to his car. "I was thinking we could go for a coffee and get to know each other a bit better—you know, since we're supposed to be in love, and all. Work on that back story of ours."

Why does that make me blush? I never blush. I'm the one who makes guys blush! I clear my throat and nod. "Yeah, sure. I mean... I was going to study, but..."

Damon's eyebrows arch.

I shrug. "Whatever. I can study later."

What is it about the Princes of Farcliff that makes us girls go all gooey? Elle is wrapped around Prince Charlie's little finger, and I'm basically salivating at the mere sight of Prince Damon.

It's not like me.

He opens the car door for me, which makes me blush even harder. I put my backpack down at my feet and watch the Prince as he walks around the front of the car toward the driver's side. He carries himself with his shoulders thrown back and his head held high, as if he owns the ground he walks on.

Which, I guess he does, in a way.

When the Prince slips inside the car, I inhale the scent of his cologne and my heart skips. I didn't notice that when he was at my house. His scent is fresh and earthy, and it makes me want to bury my head in his chest. My eyes drop down to his hand on the gear stick and I watch the way his muscular forearm flexes a bit. A flutter passes through my chest.

I guess I'm a forearm kind of girl—I hadn't realized that until I saw the ones attached to Prince Damon's body. He glances at me and smiles before starting the car.

"There's a quiet café about ten minutes away. We can go somewhere closer, but I'm afraid we won't have time to talk to each other if people start recognizing me." He pinches his lips and his cheeks turn pink, as if he's embarrassed that he's famous.

I grin. "Ten minutes is fine."

We drive in silence for a couple of minutes. Then, the Prince glances at me. "I like your hair."

"*Nothing in this world is harder than speaking the truth, nothing easier than flattery.*"

"What?"

I look over at him, shaking my head and grinning. "Sorry. It's a quote by Dostoyevsky. It pops into my head whenever someone gives me a random compliment in an awkward situation."

"Is this an awkward situation?"

I think for a moment. "Not exactly awkward. Unusual, maybe."

"Do you always quote Russian novelists?"

"Only when it's appropriate." I glance over to see a grin on his face. My heart thumps. "What about you?"

"Do I quote Russian novelists?"

"No," I laugh. "Have you ever dyed your hair."

Prince Damon chuckles. "No. It wouldn't exactly be appropriate princely behavior, as my father loves to say."

I scoff. "What about your brother Charlie? He has tattoos from head to toe. Is that 'princely'?"

"He and I are pretty different."

"Mmm," I say. I glance out the window and try to still my beating heart. Is the Prince doing this to me? Am I nervous?

Let's get one thing straight: Dahlia Raventhal does *not* get nervous around guys. I make *them* nervous. I bring guys home whenever I want! I'm the one who has *them* begging for more—and this whole good-guy act that Prince Damon has going on isn't my thing.

I like guys with a little edge. Not goodie-two-shoes princes giving up their royal privileges to study medicine.

So, why is my pulse so erratic?

I hear the Prince take a deep breath and I can feel his gaze on me. I close my eyes for a moment and smooth my hands over my black leggings. By the time we get to the café, my palms are sweaty and my mouth is dry.

I'm definitely nervous.

I shouldn't be with him. His family had my mother thrown out of the Kingdom. They're the reason I didn't even know my last name until I was sixteen years old.

My mother warned me about the Farcliff family, but seeing how Charlie cares about Elle, and meeting Damon makes me suspect that my aunt Theresa is right. Maybe there's nothing to worry about. What happened with my mother was a long time ago.

Maybe this dinner party is the best thing that's ever happened to me. Maybe it's my opportunity to find out the truth—and in the process, get rid of this silly superstition about a curse.

Plus, Prince Damon has a point. We need to come up with a good back story if we're going to convince the King that we're in love.

When we arrive, the Prince opens the car door for me again to get out, and holds the café door open for me, too. Mr. Goodie-Two-Shoes is a gentleman, apparently.

Not my thing. I'm definitely not into him.

Still, I smile at him, ducking my head as I walk inside. The café is cozy and quiet, with fabric draped over the ceiling and dim, colorful lamps on every table. It looks like a boho dream.

I grin. "I like this place."

"I thought you might," Damon replies. His eyes twinkle

and it makes my heart do that funny flip again. "Here." He leads me to a low table in the corner with a bunch of cushions around it. We sit down, Damon lounging and stretching his long legs across to the other end of the table. He leans on one elbow, flicking those bright, blue eyes up at me.

We stare at each other for a moment, and my mouth goes dry. I lick my lips and his eyes follow the movement. Heat teases the edges of my stomach and I clear my throat.

"So—this dinner. What's that about?"

Damon sighs. "My father is worried about Charlie. He's got this idea in his head that Charlie has to marry a suitable wife, but he and Charlie don't exactly see eye to eye about the definition of 'suitable'. We just have to throw him off the scent."

The Prince's lips tug upward in a mischievous kind of grin. My insides melt.

There's a spark in Prince Damon's eye that I didn't expect to see. Something that says there's more to him than they write in the papers.

Or maybe I'm just hoping there is, because my body is rebelling against me.

He's one hundred percent *not* my type. Prince Damon always has his hair cut short, he's clean-shaven, and he's a star student. He ticks all the boxes that he's supposed to tick.

Me, on the other hand? If someone asks me to tick a box, I usually end up covering the page in glitter. I've managed to make it into one of the best microbiology programs on the continent at Farcliff University, but I'm far from conventional.

Yet, here, in this bohemian café, with Prince Damon sending heat zipping up and down my body, I can't help but wonder if I'm wrong about him. What secrets does he keep hidden in the depths of his heart? What sharp edges does he have that haven't quite been blunted by the royal life?

A blush creeps up my cheeks and I take a deep breath. I can't think like this. Prince Damon is off-limits. All of Farcliff royalty is off-limits. My mother was thrown out of this Kingdom over fifteen years ago, and she's never missed an opportunity to tell me how dangerous it is to get involved with royalty. She wasn't happy about me coming to Farcliff University in the first place.

But my mother isn't here, is she?

It's just me and the Prince.

"So, our back story." I tear my eyes away from his. "We met at the Prince's Ball."

"I saw you across the room and I had to have you." His eyes do that thing again, where they spark and then darken, and my whole body thrums. My blood pulses between my thighs and I clear my throat.

Prince Damon definitely has some sharp edges—the kind of edges that make me want to slice my own heart wide open.

One of the café workers brings us our drinks, and I use the opportunity to take a deep breath to compose myself. I bury my face in my coffee and try to get my thoughts in order.

I can't get involved with Prince Damon—even if he's broad-chested, sexy, and strong. Even if he looks at me like he wants to devour me.

Even if I'm dying for him to do it.

"So, Dahlia, something I've been wondering..." Prince Damon clears his throat. His cheeks flush slightly and he avoids my eyes. "You seem to have an unconventional take on clothing."

I look down at myself. "What do you mean? I'm just wearing leggings and a sweatshirt. It's basically the Farcliff University girl uniform."

"Well, maybe I should say lack of clothing." His eyes flick up to mine and it's my turn to blush.

I try to play it off, rolling my eyes and waving my hand. "Don't be so uptight, Your Highness. I swear, people in Farcliff think seeing someone without clothing is the most shocking thing in the world. Have you never seen anyone naked before?"

"Nobody like you." His voice is a low growl, and it sends a flame scorching down my spine. "Not before I even know their name."

"Well, you did know my name," I grin. My heart is thumping. I can play the bad-girl act, I can pretend like the thought of being naked with Prince Damon is no big deal, but I'd be lying. The way he's looking at me right now makes me feel more naked than I've felt in a long time. I shrug, even though my face feels hot and red. "I don't see the big deal. It's just a naked body. It's natural."

"If only more people thought like you," he chuckles.

I bite my lip. "Well, you know, I don't exactly make it a habit of letting people see me naked. But if I'm in my own house, I'll do as I please, and I refuse to be made to feel bad about it." My eyes drill into his.

Not that I feel bad right now—quite the opposite, actually. I slide my eyes over the Prince's lounging body and find myself wondering what he looks like without any clothes on.

He flashes another smile at me and I blush... *again*.

"Look, I don't think that topic is going to come up at the royal dinner table," I say as I take a sip of coffee. "Why don't we talk about other things? Favorite color? Favorite movie? Life plans? Those are the things we should be covering. Back story, remember?"

The Prince waves a hand. "My father won't be interested in any of that. As long as you stroke his ego a little, he'll believe anything you tell him."

"So why am I here?" I grin. "I thought we were supposed

to get to know each other better so that we could convince the King we were dating."

"I might have made that up." The Prince laughs and my insides melt. "I just wanted to get to know you for myself."

There it is again—that blush. I swear, I have never blushed so much in my life. Ask Elle—I'm usually great with men. I see one that I like, and I go for him.

But Prince Damon has me feeling upside down. He drags his eyes over my body and sends my head spinning. He makes my fingers itch to touch his skin, to feel his body against mine.

I'm attracted to his freaking forearms, for Farcliff's sake.

I reel my thoughts back in again. I can't be thinking like that. This is just to help Elle. It's a one-time dinner. I'm not actually getting involved with the Prince. I'm not dating him.

Dating a prince when you're living your life with an unbreakable curse is a recipe for disaster.

I'll do this for Elle, I'll get as much information about my mother as possible, and then I'll never go to the castle again.

Easy, right?

4

—————

## DAMON

WHEN I DROP Dahlia back off at the campus library, I watch her walk away and adjust my pants for the thousandth time. It's a miracle I can walk, or talk, or think, or do *anything* when all the blood in my body is occupied with one particular appendage. I swallow, unsure of exactly what I'm getting myself into.

The Raventhals have a long history with the Farcliff family. Tabitha Raventhal—Dahlia's mother—was my mother's best friend. Then my mother died, and Lady Raventhal started making all kinds of accusations against my father— accusations that included murder. That didn't go down well.

As a result, I've always been told that the Raventhals are bad people.

But talking to Dahlia, learning about her studies, about her growing up with her aunts in the Rocky Mountains—it doesn't seem like the upbringing of a bad person. It seems like the upbringing of a very wholesome, intelligent girl.

My mother's death was the beginning of the end for me. I was young, but that's when I learned that there's badness inside of me.

29

Inside Dahlia, though? I don't see any.

I need to know more—and, fuck it, Charlie's already dating someone he shouldn't. Why not me? I'm not even in line for the throne! I should be able to do whatever I want.

I head straight to the Farcliff National Library, near the center of the city. The library sits on the same streets as the court, the city council, and the main cathedral. All three institutions are cornerstones of Farcliff Kingdom, and all three of them sit in the shadow of the castle.

I glance up at the castle—at my home—rising high above the entire Kingdom. I bite my lip.

My father, as he grows older, is getting more aggressive. He's not getting along with Charlie, and he seems to be unwilling to surrender his power.

Throwing Dahlia Raventhal into the mix isn't a good idea.

But... I can't quite bring myself to care. I've always been the perfect son, the perfect Prince, the perfect everything. I've kept my own suffering private, away from prying eyes, like a good Prince. I've done everything I'm supposed to do.

So what if I pursue this girl? At least I can find out who she really is.

But I need to know exactly what kind of ripples this will cause with my father. I was young when my mother died— only eight years old. The memories of that night still haunt my dreams, and try as I might to keep them buried, they're never quite gone.

There's still the voice in my head that says it was all my fault.

I need to put that voice to bed, and the only way to do that is to discover the truth about what happened to my mother. Meeting Dahlia almost seems like a sign that it's time for me to face my past head-on.

Plus, there's a part of me—not a small part, either—wants

to know more about Dahlia. She's unlike anyone I've ever met, from her hair, to her laugh, to her unique perspective on nudity.

A unique-*good* perspective, that is.

So, with a deep breath, I push the National Library doors open and I make my way toward the back of the library. The head librarian, Mrs. Hill, is at the front desk as usual. The elderly woman's gravity-defying glasses are perched on the end of her nose. She glances at me and gives me a small nod. She's used to me. I like coming here to study whenever I need a break from the castle. My usual study space is on the fifth floor of the National Library, in a little hidden corner that no one ever visits.

This time, though, I don't go up the stairs—I go down. The Archives are in the basement. The sound of my steps is muted as I make my way down the narrow stairwell. It smells stuffy and old down here, and the air is heavy with history and forgotten stories. I make my way to the microfilm machine, where all the old newspapers are kept on file. Nothing has been digitized yet, so it's a painfully slow process to do any kind of research.

Settling into a chair, I take a deep breath. I know this will take a while. I don't even really know what I'm looking for. I just know I need to know more.

More about Dahlia. More about Tabitha Raventhal. More about my mother. Talking about her at the castle is almost taboo, and her death left a dark patch in my heart that never really healed.

*It was my fault*, the Darkness inside me says. The words echo in my mind until I shake them away.

I start flicking through the microfilm reader, starting around the time of my mother's death. My throat tightens as I read the headlines about her passing. My eyes mist up as I see the grief in all the articles and reports about her life.

She was loved by everyone.

I dab at my eyes, feeling old wounds being ripped open as I think of my childhood, and how difficult my mother's passing was. I find myself reading article, after article, after article, smiling and letting the tears fall down my cheeks as I read how beloved the Queen had been.

As I flick through the newspapers, the headlines start to change. They take a sharp turn when Tabitha goes public with her accusations of murder. I'm perched on the edge of my seat, scanning the headlines and trying to untangle what exactly happened.

After a couple of dozen articles, a clear picture starts to emerge from the newspaper reports and editorials. My mother died mysteriously, and the official autopsy never revealed a conclusive cause of death. My throat tightens and I push down memories of the night she died.

Tabitha Raventhal went on the record accusing the rest of the royal family—the King of Farcliff included—of murder.

She claimed to have compelling evidence, but that evidence was never revealed.

Aunt Malerie, my father's sister, denounced her claims and called for her to be exiled. Tabitha Raventhal was disgraced, accused of desecrating the Queen's memory, and banished from Farcliff.

No Raventhal set foot in Farcliff for fifteen years.

Until now.

When my back starts to ache and my neck feels stiff, I lean back and stretch my head from side to side. I inhale as my mind spins circles around me.

I never knew about any of this. How could I? I was barely eight years old. All I remember was that I'd been terribly sad, and everything was confusing. It was the start of a dark, downward spiral that I never really recovered from. I threw myself into school, sure, but the pain is still there, buried underneath it all.

I've dealt with that pain in my own way. I have the bruises on my ribs and scars on my back to prove it. I keep them covered, so no one can see what I do to myself, but I know they're there. Scars help me remember what it's like to dive head-first into sharp, pulsing pain. They help me remember what it's like to feel release.

Sighing, I flick through the archived newspapers again, trying to glean any sort of truth about the Raventhal accusations.

The only thing I learn is that Tabitha Raventhal was largely ridiculed and accused of stirring up controversy. Any explanation as to *why* she would make those accusations was never provided. I suspect a lot of the news reports were influenced by the Crown—by my father, and possibly Aunt Mal, as well. Judging by how much the King wanted to shut down any talk of my mother's death as I grew up, I can only imagine how desperate he was to stop these news stories from spreading.

I didn't mind. I didn't want to talk about my mother's death, either.

In all these archives, there's nothing about Dahlia. Nothing about a daughter, and no mention of Tabitha's children. I frown, flicking back through the microfilm a few years. Dahlia is probably, what? Twenty-one? Maybe twenty-two?

It takes me another half-hour to find anything about Dahlia, and when I do, my breath catches in my throat. I lean over the microfilm machine as my heart thumps harder. There's a grainy picture of Tabitha Raventhal and a little bundle in her arms that I assume is Dahlia. She's standing next to my mother, and the three of us boys. I'm staring at the camera with wide eyes—I'm probably no older than three years old.

I release my clenched breath. I don't even know why I'm relieved. Maybe because Dahlia exists? Because Tabitha did indeed have a daughter? Dahlia's parentage, at least, isn't a lie?

The picture is her christening. My mother was named godmother, apparently. There are three other women there—Dahlia's aunts. I flick to the next frame of the microfilm and my eyebrows arch. Aunt Malerie wasn't happy about not being invited to the christening, apparently. There's a whole article about her reaction.

I lean back in my chair and exhale. Even through old newspaper articles, I can sense the tension between my mother, Tabitha Raventhal, and Malerie Farcliff. It's palpable in these stories—but I still can't really gather any meaningful information from them.

All I know is Tabitha and Aunt Mal didn't like each other, but what else is new? Aunt Mal's always had a short fuse and a mean temper.

I start searching the files for anything else about Dahlia, but I come up empty. It's like she disappeared from the public record when she was just a baby.

Then, the sound of voices makes my spine stiffen.

"Just down here, dear," Mrs. Hill's voice comes down the corridor. Her shoes clack on the hard floor, growing louder as she nears.

Another muffled voice sounds, and I stare at the door. My heart thumps, and I flick the microfilm away from the article I was reading. I shuffle my notes and stuff them into my shirt pocket, smoothing my clothes down and trying to still the thumping of my heart.

It feels like I'm doing something wrong. Like I shouldn't be here, and I shouldn't be reading about these things...

...but why? I'm the son of the King of Farcliff, and if anyone has the right to be down here, it's me.

Mrs. Hill's voice is near now, and it's only a matter of seconds before the door opens. I jump out of my chair and grab my jacket, ready to brush past the newcomers on my way out.

The door opens and Mrs. Hill comes through with none other than Dahlia Raventhal.

"Oh! Your Highness! I thought you'd be on the fifth floor, as usual. If I'd known..."

"It's fine, Mrs. Hill." I nod to Dahlia. "Miss Raventhal."

She curtsies, and my lips tug at the corners. Seeing her behave like a proper lady is the diametric opposite of how she'd been at her own house—naked and casual and unashamedly herself.

Mrs. Hill mutters a few more words until I send her away with a nod. Dahlia shifts her weight from foot to foot, biting her lip and staring at the microfilm reader.

I wait for her to speak, but she says nothing.

Finally, I clear my throat. "What are you doing here? I don't think there's much about microbiology in the Archives."

Dahlia's cheeks flush pink and she lifts her eyes up to mine. She takes a deep breath, tucking a strand of lavender hair behind her ear.

"I was coming to find out about my mother... and the Queen. What are you doing here?"

A grin tugs at my lips and I chuckle gently. "Same, actually. Reading up on you."

"Anything interesting?" Dahlia throws her bag down on the floor and strips her jacket off, tossing it onto a chair. A low growl rumbles through my chest and I want nothing more than to tear her clothes off and take her right here, right now.

With my hands itching to touch her and my tongue dying to taste her, I just swallow and shake my head. "Apart from the news of your birth and your christening, you don't exist in Farcliff archives."

Dahlia grins. "Just the way I like it. I'm a woman of mystery." She walks up beside me, her arm brushing mine as she leans over the microfilm reader. She glances back at me as a shy smile stretches over her lips. "You don't mind me being here?"

I shake my head. "Not at all." Surprisingly, it's the truth.

Dahlia smiles at me, and a bolt of lightning passes through my chest. Up until two days ago, I didn't even know this girl existed. Now, she's everywhere...

...and I like it. A lot.

# 5

# DAHLIA

Note to self: avoid confined spaces with Damon Farcliff.

His presence is intoxicating. His body is big, and broad, and it's calling out to the primal side of me. He fills up the room that we're in, his aura pressing against me and making me feel like all the oxygen in the world wouldn't be enough to fill my lungs.

I haven't had sex in days, and I'm starting to feel it. The ache between my legs is almost unbearable. Ever since he walked through my front door, no other man seems like enough. Usually, I'm into one-night stands. I love the passing nature of them—the quiet understanding that it's temporary.

This week, though? The thought of a one-night stand bores me.

Damon, on the other hand, doesn't. What I feel around him is the opposite of boredom. It's electric and addictive.

I try to focus on the headlines on the microfilm in front of me, but my mind keeps drifting to his arm, and how it brushes against mine. To his spicy, fresh scent. To the sound of his voice, the low timbre of it that makes something deep in my stomach tremble with need.

This isn't supposed to happen. I'm only supposed to be doing Elle a favor. It's just one dinner, and then I go back to my regular life. I'm not supposed to be reading up on Prince Damon or trying to find out what exactly happened between his mother and my own.

Going to the castle is bad enough. My mother would have a fit if she found out. It was difficult enough to tell her I was going to Farcliff University. She made me promise to stay away from the castle.

I successfully avoided the Prince's Ball by sending Elle in my stead—but I can't avoid this dinner without letting my best friend down.

The thing is, I don't *want* to avoid this dinner. Aunt Theresa is right—I need to find my own way in life, and figure out what happened for myself. I can't live in the shadow of a curse that probably doesn't exist.

A curse! How stupid! Why I've let myself believe that my entire existence is cursed, I don't know. Maybe it's an easy excuse whenever something goes wrong.

Maybe Theresa's right—I'm just clumsy.

"What do you know about my mother's death?" Damon asks, pulling me from my thoughts.

I glance over at him and take a deep breath. "Not much. I know my mother thought it was suspicious. I know it messed her up for a long time, and she never really recovered from what happened. She sent me away when I was a baby because of the tension at the castle, apparently."

"Everybody was shocked when it happened."

I sigh. "Yeah. *Death is an old joke, but it comes like new to everyone.*"

"Dostoyevsky?" Prince Damon's eyebrow arches.

"Ivan Turgenev."

"I haven't heard of him," the Prince says with a grin.

"Stick around me long enough, and you'll learn." I laugh, nudging him.

He tilts his head . "How's your mother doing now?"

I shrug. "She's scared of everything. She gets sick really often. I don't know," I smile sadly, shaking my head. "I'm supposed to be a scientist, and I study microbiology, but sometimes I think there's more to it than that. Like her spirit is sick, or something."

"Well, medicine is an inexact science. That's what my professors always say."

I nod and turn to the microfilm. "I guess so."

Damon grunts, flicking through the archives to show me one article. "I found this. It says your mother was kicked out, but nothing about you except your christening. After that, you disappear."

"I mean, as far as Farcliff is concerned, I did disappear. I was taken away from here when I was a baby. I was sent to live with my aunts in the Rockies, like I told you earlier. My mother always said it was for my own safety, but I was never really able to figure out why."

"Hence why you're here, asking all kinds of dangerous questions" he says, smiling.

"Hence why I'm here," I repeat. "Trying to figure out how dangerous these questions are."

"Well, I can't say that I've made any discoveries." Damon says, slumping into a chair and letting his eyes drift over me. "I feel like I should know more about my own past."

"Tell me about it," I snort. "That's literally the story of my life. I didn't even know I was a Raventhal until my sixteenth birthday."

"Yeah?"

"Yep." I lean back against the desk and Prince Damon's eyes drill through me. A delicious tendril of heat follows his gaze as it passes over my body. I flush.

I turn to the archives again, mostly to avoid his gaze.

"It's probably not the type of thing that would be on the public record. You know, royal scandals and intrigue and the Queen's best friend being banished. Not to mention the King's own sister stirring shit up—which, by the way, I only found out about two days ago."

Prince Damon catches my hand. The touch surprises me and makes me turn to look at him. When he pulls to bring me closer, I let him. Even though he's sitting and I'm standing, we're almost the same height. His hand drifts to my thighs, his legs caging me in on either side.

Words die on my lips. His gaze pins me in place, and I soak up the feeling he's giving me.

The Prince's scent is making my head spin. His gaze is making me hot, and my thoughts are a muddled mess. I came here for answers, but all I've gotten are more questions—and I don't hate it. When he looks at me this way, it makes me want more than just his eyes on my body.

He lifts his fingers up to my cheek. I lean into his hand, exhaling gently as he cups my cheek. I close my eyes.

"You're beautiful, Dahlia Raventhal."

"I'm not supposed to talk to you."

"Says who?"

"My entire family."

"They're not here, are they?"

A smile tugs at the corners of my lips and I open my eyes again. His lips are plump, and pink, and kissable. I lift my hands to his shoulders, playing with the edge of his collar.

"For the record," he says in a gravelly voice, "I'm not supposed to talk to you, either."

"Says who?"

"My entire family," he answers with a grin.

"So, why are you?"

"Because I want to." His hand curls into the nape of my neck and he pulls me closer. I catch myself on his shoulders, leaning my forehead against his.

Everything in my mind is telling me to back away, to abort this whole dinner, to run, run, run. I grew up fearing the Farcliff family—I'm not supposed to kiss one of them.

Prince Damon tilts his head and brushes his lips over mine, and a sizzle of energy passes through me. My hands curl into the fabric of his shirt and I find myself leaning into him. My heart thumps. My blood feels thick and hot in my veins.

Prince Damon brushes his other hand up my leg and cups the side of my ass. My leggings are so thin it feels almost like he's touching my bare skin.

Or, maybe, I wish he was touching it.

He pulls me to him, squeezing his legs against mine and finally, *finally* kisses me.

His lips taste like fire and honey—like sin and sweetness and everything I've ever wanted. I fall into him, wrapping my arms around his neck as he pulls me onto his lap. Cupping my face, he deepens the kiss and I melt.

I burn.

I *need*.

Heat explodes inside of me. My heart thumps against my ribcage and I moan into his mouth as he swipes his tongue between my lips. I'm trembling, clinging onto his neck as his touch sets me aflame.

The Prince's hands slip under my shirt and his touch marks me. I know I'll feel it for days.

It feels wrong and so, so right. In the basement of the

National Library Archives, I kiss Prince Damon with all the heat of my desire. The voice in my head telling me to stop gets quieter and quieter, until all I can hear is the pumping of my blood in my ears.

Prince Damon growls. It's a strong, rumbling sound in the depths of his chest. He pulls me closer to him. His hand trails down my spine and I melt into him, his mouth claiming me again and again—and I let him.

No, I don't let him. I beg it of him. I tangle my hands into his hair and arch my back into him and let my body scream *take me*.

I want this. I can't deny it. I've wanted this from the first moment the Prince walked in my front door. I've wanted his hands on my skin, his lips on mine.

And I still want more.

Curling his fingers into my hair, Prince Damon tilts my head back and leaves a trail of fiery kisses down my neck. He brushes his lips over my collarbone, sending shivers of plea-sure teasing through my body.

He kisses the center of my chest, between my breasts and then back up again. I sigh, closing my eyes and relishing the heat of his touch.

We're alone down here—so alone. No one will come here, and the hesitation in my mind evaporates.

I want him. Badly.

I lift my leg up and straddle Prince Damon, arching my spine and then rolling my hips toward him. His hands slide down to cup my ass as another growl rumbles through his chest.

I love this—*us*. I love the rawness and the closeness of it. I love the feeling of his strong, possessive hands as they brand me. I love the taste of his skin, his scent.

Doubts be damned. Family history? What history? Who cares about the past, when the present is so damn good?

A moan slips through my lips and I kiss the Prince harder—and then my phone rings, and I freeze.

6

———

## DAMON

"LET IT RING," I say when Dahlia pulls away. Her lips are swollen and glistening from our kiss, and they're calling out to me again. I don't want to stop kissing her—ever.

"I can't. It's my dad." She slides off my lap. "I have a special ringtone for him. He never calls me without texting me first to make sure I'm free."

"You think something's wrong?"

"I don't know." Dahlia's lips pinch together and she leans over to rummage through her bag. Her leggings stretch over her ass and go slightly sheer. She's wearing a thong.

I clear my throat and adjust my pants as they tighten at the waist.

Dahlia answers her phone. She takes a couple of steps away and I turn my attention to the microfiche reader to give her some semblance of privacy. In this cramped basement, though, there's no such thing.

"Hey, Dad," Dahlia says, glancing at me before turning away. "What's up?" She runs her hand through her hair to try to smooth it down.

I flick through old archives, not seeing anything.

"She *what*? Is she okay?"

I glance at Dahlia, who's frozen with her hand on her forehead. Her eyes get wider and wider and they start to fill with tears.

My heart thumps. Something's wrong.

"Okay... Yeah. Why didn't you tell me?" She takes a deep breath and nods, even though her father can't see her. "Love you too. Bye."

Holding her phone in her hand for a few seconds, Dahlia stares at the floor by her feet. Then, with a deep breath, she lifts her gaze up to mine. "I have to go."

"Is everything okay?"

"It's my mom," she says, throwing her phone into her bag and slinging the backpack over her shoulder.

"Can I do anything?"

Dahlia looks at me, wide-eyed. She shakes her head. "No. I'll see you around."

"Can I see you before the dinner party?" I hate how needy I sound. I clear my throat. "I mean, we could try to find more information on what happened with our mothers."

Dahlia's face twists. "I'm not sure that's a good idea. Maybe this is a sign. I have to go."

"A sign of what?"

She steps over to me and places a hand on my shoulder, brushing her lips against my cheek. Then, without another word, she hurries down the hallway.

She's gone, and bitterness sours my stomach.

I'm alone in the National Library Archives with a boner tenting my pants. I can still taste her lips on mine. I blow out the air from my lungs, slumping back into my chair and covering my face with my hands.

That girl drives me crazy. I don't know what it is about her, but she's different...

...and completely fucking wrong for me.

Our pasts are intertwined in ways we don't even understand. I want her, and she wants me, but if we got involved with each other, would there really be a future for us? Do I want a future with Dahlia Raventhal?

When my heartbeat slows down again, I stare at the microfiche reader and frustration bubbles up inside me.

My mother's death didn't make any sense to me. All I knew at the time was that the events of that night made me feel wrong.

Guilty.

Now, my memories play tricks on me. Was I ever really there? Did I see the hatred in my father's eyes when he sent me to her? Did I really bring her that cup of tea, or am I only imagining it? I've spent so long ignoring the twisting in my gut when I think of her death, that I don't even trust my own mind to remember it.

After she died, our whole family almost fell apart. Aunt Malerie came to stay with us for a few months. I remember hating when she hugged me because she smelled like onions. I used to run away from her and my father, and stay in my room for days at a time.

My brothers and I all reacted differently. Charlie got angry. I became a recluse. Gabe was so young that he was mostly just sad and confused. It was only later, in his teens, that he became the wild child he is now.

When I threw myself into schoolwork, it helped. I started having dreams of being a doctor and being able to save my mother, and I decided that's what I wanted to do—royal duties be damned. I can never go back and save my mother, but maybe I can save someone else.

I squeeze my eyes shut and bury my chin in my chest. This dream of going to medical school... Is that a way for me to atone for what happened to my mother that night?

*What did I do to her?*

Inhaling sharply, I straighten up and interlace my fingers over my head. My heart is thumping. Sweat beads on my neck, a drop of it trailing all the way down my spine. I suck another breath in through my teeth and try to contain my swirling thoughts.

I was eight years old. I was a child. I can't be guilty if I don't even know what I'm guilty of doing.

The tightness in my chest eases, and I talk myself down from the ledge.

I've always felt like there's something missing from my life, like I was robbed from some universal experience that everyone with a mother has. The only thing that ever makes that feeling go away is pain.

Pain... and the feeling I get when I'm with Dahlia. She's the only one that makes me feel like things aren't all wrong, like life isn't some long, drawn-out, awful joke.

What was it Dahlia said about a joke? *Death is an old joke, but it comes like new to everyone.*

It doesn't feel like a joke right now.

My mother's death was swept under the rug. Now, I'm here on my own, looking through old newspaper clippings for any clue as to what really happened over fifteen years ago. I'm trying to untangle the memories of my eight-year-old self, wondering if it was all a dream. What kind of sense does that make?

My blood pumps harder and I slam my hand down on the microfiche reader. I let out a yell in the silent, stuffy space and slam my hand down again.

Gulping down deep breaths, I try to regain control of myself. I know this feeling. I'm on a precipice, and if the darkness wins, it's a long, hard fall to the bottom. If I keep spiraling, I'll need a release. I'll need bright, sharp agony to relieve the pressure building inside me.

I slam the base of my hand against the side of my head, grunting as pain explodes across my temple. Once, twice, three times I hit myself. My thoughts stop spiraling and I can breathe again.

Pain has always helped get me back on track. It's not that I enjoy hurting myself, but it jars my mind back into line. Whenever I need it, pain is my most reliable companion. With another deep breath, I'm able to think clearly again.

I take stock of my surroundings—at the archives, the books, the microfilm, at my jacket on the floor. I start to calm down.

I'll do what I can to find out what happened to my mother. And when I do, I'll know why Dahlia is so hesitant about coming to the castle. I'll know what happened between our families, and where the bad blood stems.

I'll know if I need to blame myself, and I'll find out if I should stay away from Dahlia.

Snorting to myself, I shake my head and stare at the ceiling.

Who am I kidding? I'm going to pursue her no matter what. The instant I saw the multicolored bush between her legs, I knew I wanted to dive head-first into it. I'll chase after her to the ends of the earth. I'll uncover whatever happened between our families, and while I'm at it, I'll make Dahlia mine.

That girl doesn't know it yet, but she's woken something up in me that isn't going to go away. I need her like I need air.

Seeing her is the breath in my lungs. Tasting her is all the sustenance I need.

Dahlia Raventhal may have the wrong last name—but I don't care, because she's the one I want.

# 7

# DAHLIA

MY SUITCASE IS HALF-PACKED when my father calls again. I'm sweaty, worried, and my mind is racing. I can't even begin to process the kiss with Prince Damon.

"You're packing, aren't you?" My father chides.

"I need to be there, Dad. If Mom is in the hospital, I need to go."

She fell down a short flight of stairs and broke her hip—probably at the exact moment I was locking lips with Prince Damon. It's the curse—I know it is. Whenever I think something good is on the verge of happening, my life starts to crumble to pieces.

"What you need to do is make sure you do well on your midterms," my father says. "You need to focus on school and not worry about your mother. She doesn't need surgery, and she's doing fine."

"You should have called me sooner."

"I didn't want to worry you."

"All you've done is make me feel even worse about not being there. What happened?"

"Your aunt called after her visit with you." My father takes a deep breath. "She... She told your mother that she encouraged you to go to the castle. You know how your mom feels about that..."

"So, Mom freaked out because I'm in Farcliff? Again?"

"Dahlia, listen to me." My father takes a deep breath, and I can imagine him pinching the bridge of his nose. "Your mother didn't want you to go back to Farcliff, but I convinced her to let you go because I think it's what's best for you. You need to make your own way in this world and stop letting the past hold you back."

"What past, Dad? All I know is that I was sent away from here years ago, and I spent fifteen years in the fucking forest with my aunts! I don't even know what happened with mom when she was in Farcliff. I don't know anything about the past."

My father sighs. "First of all, watch your language, Dahlia. Second... Listen, when you come back to visit, I'll tell you everything. Until then, you need to do well at school, and not worry about your mother."

"Dad..."

"Dahlia, I'm serious."

I throw one last shirt in my suitcase and sink down to the floor. "You promise you'll tell me everything about Mom and the Queen?"

"I promise."

"*Everything*?"

"Yes, Dahlia, everything. Now unpack your suitcase. I'll call you tonight from the hospital, and you can speak to your mother. Just... Don't mention anything about the royal family."

I bite my lip. My mother accidentally broke her hip because of the mere idea that my aunt would encourage me to go to the castle. What if she found out I was going for a private dinner party?

What if she found out I *kissed Prince-freaking-Damon?*

I take a deep breath. "Okay, talk to you later. Love you, Dad."

"Love you too, kiddo."

I hang up the phone and flop down onto my bed. My roommate, Elle, pokes her head in. Her eyebrow arches.

"Going somewhere?"

"No."

"You just pack your suitcase for fun?"

"I like to be prepared."

Elle grins. "You weirdo."

"Weird people are the best people."

She laughs and then tilts her head to the side. "Prince Damon seemed pretty into you yesterday."

"What makes you say that?" I answer, averting my eyes. I tuck a strand of hair behind my ear and get off my bed again, turning to my suitcase. "I thought he was pretty casual."

"Casually checking you out as if he's been stuck on a desert island, and you're the first woman he's seen in ten years. If that's what you meant, then yeah, I'd say it was pretty casual."

"It's not like that," I respond, waving a hand. "I'm just doing this for you."

"And I appreciate it, Dahlia. More than I can say."

"How are things going between you and Prince Charlie?"

Elle sits on the bed and watches me unpack my suitcase. She folds her arms behind her head and stares at the ceiling, sighing.

"That bad, huh?" I grin.

"No, they're that *good*. It's perfect. I mean, it's too perfect.

What am I doing, Dahlia? I should be focusing on my studies, and on the rowing team. Not some doomed relationship."

"You keep saying that," I smile. "Whether you think it's doomed, or you think it isn't, you'll end up being right either way."

Elle nods her head and my thoughts flick back to Prince Damon.

Maybe I should take my own advice. Every time I'm in the same room as him, he sucks the air out of my lungs. He makes me blush, and laugh, and makes my whole body burn up.

But... it can't be real. I'm a Raventhal. My family was exiled. How could I possibly have a future with Prince Damon?

I'm like Elle—completely, utterly doomed.

Elle is talking, but I don't hear a word of it. I put the last of my clothes back in my dresser and take a moment to compose myself.

I am a sexually liberated, open and honest young woman. I do what I want. So how come one little itty-bitty kiss with Prince Damon has me thinking about a future with him? I practically have baby names picked out and everything.

This isn't me.

"What do you think?" Elle says, leaning her head on her fist.

I snap my head toward her. "Sorry, I missed that last part. What did you say?"

"I knew you were a million miles away. What are you thinking about?"

"It's nothing," I say, forcing a smile. And I mean it. It's nothing. Whatever happened with Prince Damon, and whatever happens at this dinner party, it means nothing. It's going nowhere. It's bad enough that I've come back to Farcliff—my mother can hardly handle the thought of it.

Before I get involved with anything to do with Prince Damon—before I even think about it—I need to know the truth about what happened between his mother and mine.

"What should I wear to this dinner party?"

Elle scoffs. "Don't ask me. You're the fashionista here. I live in sports bras and sweat pants." She flashes a smile at me and I laugh.

She's right. Elle is an athletic, no-nonsense person—the last thing she thinks about is fashion. I practically had to force her to wear a dress for the Prince's Ball last month.

"I was thinking something a bit more demure," I say, opening my closet.

"Do you own anything demure? I've only ever seen you look like a rainbow."

I throw her a glance over my shoulder and purse my lips. "I'll have you know my wardrobe is very versatile."

"Oh yeah? You had me fooled." Elle laughs.

I try to go back to how things were in my mind before today—before the kiss. I try to let my shoulders relax and not worry about this dinner party at the castle, not think about who the royal family are or what they did to my mother...

...or to the Queen.

But I can't.

Questions fly around my head until I feel dizzy. If Elle notices that something's wrong, she doesn't say anything. She's probably too busy worrying about her own whirlwind romance with Prince Charlie.

At least she has a romance to speak of. I've only kissed Prince Damon once, for Farcliff's sake. I force a smile and drag Elle back to the living room, where we stuff ourselves with food and watch bad TV until our brains turn to mush.

When she goes to bed, I lay back on the couch and listen to the silence of the night. I decide that whatever this feeling for Prince Damon is, it's wrong. Even if there is a spark between us, I can't pursue it.

Not until I know the truth about what happened with our mothers. Not until I know it's safe for me and my family in Farcliff. Not until I shake this stupid curse, and I know that I won't put my mother in the hospital by seeing him.

But when I close my eyes, I see the Prince's face. I feel the whisper of his lips over mine, and my skin burns where he touched it.

I let out a long sigh. I already know I can never have him.

8

———

**DAMON**

The NEXT TIME I see Dahlia, she's exiting the royal car that picked her up, stepping lightly up the wide palace steps.

She looks incredible. I thought Dahlia would be wearing something crazy and colorful, but instead, she's wearing a curve-hugging black gown. It's cut high on her neck, but all I'm picturing is what she looked like with nothing on. I'm dying to rip that dress off her the moment I see her.

I thought she was sexy before, but I had no idea. She's a goddess. Pretending to be interested in her tonight won't be a problem.

"You ready for this?" Charlie glances at me. His eyes are dark, and I know he's worried. If our father doesn't believe that Dahlia and I are together, Charlie will be in trouble.

But right now, as Dahlia flashes a bright smile at me, I'm not worried about Charlie at all. I extend my arm to her and she slips her hand into the crook of my arm, and nothing exists except her.

"Dahlia." I nod, pulling her a bit closer.

Her cheeks flush pink, and my heart races. A sharp

current zips down my spine and I resist the urge to run my hand down to the small of her back.

I lead her to the formal living room, where my father awaits. Dahlia does all the right things. She curtsies when she's supposed to, addresses him how she's supposed to, and never hesitates when she's speaking about her supposed relationship with me.

I just sit here, wanting her.

Before dinner even starts, I know my father believes we're really together. I catch him looking at me when I'm busy staring at Dahlia. I'm not even trying to pretend—I just can't stop looking at her. My father's brow arches and he exhales slowly, leaning back in his chair. His eyes turn back to Dahlia.

"Studying chemistry, was it?" The King asks.

"Microbiology," she responds. Dahlia's hands are folded on her lap and her back is straight as a rod. Apparently, her aunts in Colorado gave her formal etiquette training while living in the woods. I'd have never guessed that she grew up with only her aunts and forest animals as company. I'd have guessed she was raised in a palace like this one.

I take a seat next to her and she leans into me ever so slightly, as if there's a magnetic attraction between us. It feels right having her beside me. My fingers itch to slip that dress off her body and run my hands over every bit of her. The thought of dragging my tongue between her thighs makes my cock throb.

I'm not sure she feels the same way. Other than saying and doing all the right things, Dahlia doesn't give me any sign that she'd like a repeat of what happened in the archives. She's distant, and I don't like it.

As the conversation moves away from Dahlia and on to current events, I see Charlie breathe a sigh of relief. We might actually pull this off. If Father believes that Dahlia and I are together, it gives Charlie a chance to figure his own shit out.

We're past the hard part—getting my father comfortable. Now all we need to do is make it through a twelve-course dinner. As long as my father has a few more glasses of wine, everything should be fine.

He'll think Dahlia and I are together. He might even want to invite her back to the castle, which would mean I'd get to see her again.

Who knows how long this charade will have to last? How many more times will Charlie and Elle need us to pretend?

Hopefully many, many times, if I get my way.

I lean back in the sofa, my eyes drifting over to Dahlia again. Her fingers are curled around a wine glass, her lips barely touching the edge of it. She's wearing soft, pink gloss, and I wish I could taste her lips again. A smile drifts over my face, and all my worries about the past—about my mother, about Dahlia's mother, all that controversy—start to drift away.

For the first time in years, I start to feel like I'm at peace.

It's all in the past, and maybe we can build our own future together. Who cares about intrigue and royal plots? Who cares about something that happened fifteen years ago? What about the here and now? What about this... whatever-it-is between us? What about Dahlia and me, wanting each other?

Isn't that more important than some stupid family feud?

But then, the living room door opens and every set of eyebrows in the room arches at once. My aunt Malerie steps through, dressed in a long, black, velvet gown. Her skin is deathly pale, and she looks at us all one by one.

"Mal," the King says as he heaves himself out of his chair.

"What a surprise! We weren't expecting you back until summer."

Her eyes swing around the room, coming to rest on Dahlia. A chill runs down my spine, and Dahlia shivers, too. I put my hand around her shoulders.

"What's this? A dinner party?" Mal's eyes swing to my father. "I'm offended I wasn't invited."

Charlie and I exchange a glance—that's Aunt Mal for you. Never attends any events, but gets upset when she isn't invited to them. She's always been this way.

"I didn't know you were in town," the King responds, waving a hand. He walks over to kiss his sister's cheeks.

Her eyes stay trained on Dahlia. "Who do we have here?"

"Auntie Mal, this is Dahlia," I say after I clear my throat. "I believe you two met a long time ago—about twenty years, give or take. She's Tabitha Raventhal's daughter."

Mal's lips tug into a smile—and not a nice one. Not that I'd ever describe Aunt Mal as 'nice'. Her lips twist into a cruel sort of smirk, and her eyes flash with malice.

"Of course," she says. "I remember your christening."

My thoughts flick to the newspaper clippings in the archives. She was offended about that christening, too—at least I know that part of the story is true.

The air in the room grows heavy until my father claps his hands and calls for the staff. "Set another place at the table for Lady Farcliff." He turns to my aunt. "Mal, tell us about your travels. You were in Canada, were you not?"

Mal glances at Dahlia for a second too long, and then nods. "Yes, on a skiing trip. Beautiful."

I glance at Charlie, trying to see what his take on this situation is. Why would she be back so early? How does this change what's going on tonight? Charlie just shrugs. His face looks a bit tighter than it did ten minutes ago, but he doesn't look worried. My father seems surprised, but not upset.

I'm the only one who seems mildly uncomfortable—mostly because of the way Aunt Mal looks at Dahlia, and because of everything I read in the archives. But I brush it off. It is unusual to have a Raventhal in Farcliff, after all.

Dahlia relaxes a bit as Malerie talks about her ski trip. Aunt Mal has been in and out of our lives for as long as I can remember. She'll go on months-long trips, sometimes gone for a year or two before reappearing in Farcliff without warning. The last time I saw her was four years ago, at Charlie's twenty-first birthday.

It's not unusual for her to pop in like this. It's just... *uncomfortable.*

For me, at least.

Her eyes swing over to me, and I can't read them. She's always taken a keen interest in me, especially after the Queen died. It's like my aunt felt responsible for me, but I've never felt entirely comfortable around her.

When the *maître d* comes to lead us to the dining room, Mal shakes her head. "I'm off again, I have business to attend to."

"You can't stay for dinner?" The King asks. "Now I'm the one who's offended."

I cough to hide my laugh.

My aunt shakes her head. She kisses all of us on both cheeks as she takes her leave. I wrinkle my nose. She still smells like onions.

When she gets to Dahlia, she keeps her hands on Dahlia's shoulders and stares into her eyes. "It was good to see you again, Miss Raventhal."

"You too, Lady Farcliff."

Mal grins, and another shiver passes down my spine.

When she's gone, I breathe a sigh of relief. I don't know why, but I'm glad she isn't staying for dinner. The way she looks at Dahlia makes the hairs on the back of my neck stand up. It makes all the alpha male instincts inside of me scream to step between them, to rip my own aunt's head off for giving Dahlia a look like that.

It makes me feel like I'm losing control, and I don't like it.

But Aunt Mal leaves, and I relax.

As the meal progresses, and the wine flows, my desire for Dahlia grows. I forget about Aunt Mal's appearance. I forget about the looks she gave me and Dahlia. I forget about the Archives, and the past, and the fact that the only reason for this dinner is Charlie's budding relationship.

All I can think of is the girl beside me. I wish I could carry her back to my bedroom and act on the feral, caveman urges that are becoming hard to contain. I don't taste any of the food, because all I could think about is tasting her.

The kiss we shared woke something inside me—something I haven't felt in a long time. I've been so focused on my studies, so focused on being the son that my mother would have wanted...

...and it feels good to feel like this. To feel something other than duty.

Don't get me wrong—I've partied. I go out with Charlie and Gabe, but my face isn't splashed across the tabloids like theirs are. I'm the studious one. The quiet one. The responsible one.

The monk who gave up his royal privileges to pursue his dream of being a doctor.

I'm the good guy.

I don't feel like being the good guy right now. I want to do every bad, dirty, filthy thing that has ever crossed my mind, and I want to do it with Dahlia.

I don't want to be quiet. I don't feel like shrinking into the shadows. Maybe it was even Mal's appearance that made me feel more protective of Dahlia. It made me feel like I need to claim her, to make her mine and make sure everyone in Farcliff knows it.

I slide my arm across the back of her chair. My father's eyebrow arches, as does Charlie's. Dahlia doesn't seem to notice. She leans into me almost instinctively again, and my heart skips a beat.

Dahlia acts like a proper lady. She knows how to speak and what fork to use for each of our twelve courses—but when she looks at me, there's a spark. That spark says *I'm like no one you've ever met.*

Maybe I'm imagining things—maybe I just want that spark to be there. But I know something special happened between us in that basement archives. That kiss was... *electric.*

This a new feeling—a pit-of-my-stomach urge to take her. An uncontrollable wave of desire.

A *need* for Dahlia Raventhal.

I glance her way every few seconds. I can't help myself.

At least it has my father convinced that she and I are together. Now, if only I could convince Dahlia to give me a chance, too.

After dinner, I walk her to the front gate.

"Thanks for coming tonight."

"I actually enjoyed it."

"You sound surprised."

"I am," Dahlia laughs.

We stand in front of each other saying nothing. Dahlia's tongue swipes across her lower lip. A driver is waiting next to a black sedan to take her back to her house, but I'm not ready to let her go.

"You want to go for a walk?"

Dahlia tilts her head. "I'm not exactly wearing appropriate footwear." She kicks out a heel to show me.

"A walk through the castle, then."

Dahlia chews her lip, hesitating. Her eyes drift over to the wide double doors behind me, and then up to the spires above us. I know she doesn't trust me, or my family. She's nervous.

But all I can do is stand here and hope that whatever I'm feeling, she feels it too.

Dahlia inhales and finally swings her eyes back to me. "Screw it. I've never been to a castle before—might as well make the most of it."

"You're telling me the daughter of Tabitha Raventhal has never been to a castle?"

"I grew up in the woods with three eccentric aunts, remember?"

I grin and hold out my arm. I wave at the driver to tell him he can relax for a few hours, and I lead Dahlia back toward the palace. She inhales sharply as we step over the threshold, squeezing my arm with hers.

"Come on, I'll show you the Great Hall." I smile and Dahlia blinks up at me. A smile slides across her lips and an irresistible flush creeps over her cheeks. She nods, and I lead her deeper into the castle.

9

——

## DAHLIA

WHATEVER RESOLVE I had to keep my distance evaporates in an instant. Prince Damon has a hold on me that I can't explain. Whenever I'm with him, I can't think logically. Every fiber of my being wants to be near him, to hear him, touch him, smell him.

To kiss him. To make love to him.

He leads me down a wide, ornate hallway. Every ten feet or so, heavy chandeliers hang from the ceiling, dripping thousands of crystals that give the whole palace an ethereal glow. The walls have carved paneling and intricate paintings dotted along the way.

When we get to the Great Hall, my breath catches in my throat. The ceiling is so high I can barely make it out. My heels clack loudly on the polished tile floors, and Prince Damon leads me out to the center of the room. He spins me in a slow circle, letting me take in the sheer size of the room. When we stand still again, my eyes come to rest on something at the far side of the room.

The throne.

Red velvet covers the broad seat and high back. It looks like it's made of solid gold.

"I've only ever seen pictures of this place," I breathe. "I had no idea it was this... rich."

"You get used to it," Damon says, shrugging. "It's the Crown's money, not mine. Not to sound ungrateful, but sometimes I wish I wasn't part of all this at all. Simple things—like who my brothers and I date—become really, really complicated."

"*Money can always and everywhere be spent, and, moreover, forbidden fruit is sweetest of all.*" I glance at the Prince as a smile tugs at his lips.

I grin. "Dostoyevsky."

"I figured," he says. "Does that make you the forbidden fruit?" Prince Damon's hands slide over my hips and he pulls me close to him. We sway from side to side in the center of the huge room as his hands drift to the small of my back.

I love how broad he is, and how strong he feels against me. How did I ever think he was a goodie-two-shoes? How did I think he was strait-laced?

Prince Damon is as bad as they come. I could taste it on his lips when we kissed. There's more to this man than I could have guessed.

My fingers trace the outline of his pecs through his white shirt, sliding up to hook around the back of the Prince's neck. He pulls me closer, so that my chest presses against his.

My whole body starts to thrum. My breath catches, and my heart thumps. Prince Damon's hands drift down to the top of my ass and I roll my hips toward him almost involuntarily.

I know I shouldn't be here. I know there's history between our two families, and I know that Prince Damon and I aren't even dating for real—it's just to help out Elle and Prince Charlie.

But right now, in the silence of the throne room, with the Prince's arms wrapped around me and my pulse thundering through my veins, it feels real. Very, very real.

"Your Highness..."

"Will you call me Damon, please? You were calling me Prince Damon and Your Highness at dinner. It's not exactly something my girlfriend would do."

"Am I your girlfriend?" I grin. "I thought we were just pretending."

"Well, we might as well pretend all the way, shouldn't we?" His voice is a low growl. His eyes darken. The Prince's hands pull me closer until my body is fused against his.

And... I like it.

This is exactly where I want to be. Even if I'm not supposed to, even if his family is supposedly dangerous. Even if my mother would have a fit if she knew where I was.

Even if I'm cursed.

Right now, none of that matters.

Prince Damon leans down and presses his lips to mine. He's gentle, soft, and slow. He teases my lips open, swiping his tongue across mine as if he's asking permission.

He doesn't need to ask. My grip on his neck tightens, and I pull him closer. I kiss him back more fiercely as my heart starts to race, thumping against my ribcage as if it's trying to escape.

The Prince's hands press harder into me, one of them sliding down to the cleft of my ass and the other sliding up my spine, sending tingles of pleasure exploding through my body. I melt into him, moaning against him as he claims my lips.

This wasn't supposed to happen. None of this was supposed to happen.

But I'm here—and I'm horny.

I want Prince Damon more than I've wanted any other man. I haven't even looked at anyone else since he walked through my front door. Elle hasn't been kept awake by my squeaking bedsprings, and I haven't had to kick anyone out of my bed in the early hours of the morning.

No, I've been too busy dreaming about the Prince. Too busy hoping to taste his lips again. Too busy imagining what he looks like without any clothes on.

Too busy wondering what it would feel like to have his cock buried deep inside me.

My fingers tangle into his hair, and his hands start to claw at the bottom of my dress. He pulls it up over my hips and grabs my bare ass with both hands.

"Fuck," he growls. "You are so perfect."

"No one is perfect," I say, nipping his bottom lip.

"Well, your ass is perfect." He gives it a squeeze and a light smack that echoes through the Great Hall.

I laugh, and Prince Damon crushes his lips to mine. He kisses me possessively as his hands stay welded to my ass. He spreads my cheeks and pulls me closer as his lips devour mine.

Electricity crackles between us. My body is on fire. I moan into his mouth and his hand flies to the nape of my neck, tilting my head back as he kisses my jaw, my neck, my collarbone.

In one smooth motion, Prince Damon picks me up and throws me over his shoulder. I yelp in surprise and he gives my ass a smack, growling. It's like we can't even manage words anymore—just wild, animalistic noises.

The Prince starts stalking toward the far end of the room,

and my heart starts to hammer. There's only one thing in the direction he's going—the throne.

"Your High—"

"Damon," he interrupts as he smacks my ass again. I inhale sharply. Pain turns to pleasure as it crackles across my skin.

"Damon," I say, looking up as he carries me. "Where are you...?"

The Prince hauls me off his shoulder and drops me down right onto the rich, red velvet of the King's throne. I gasp, trying to jump up.

"I can't—"

"*Sit*," the Prince commands. His lips crush mine again, forcing me back down onto the one chair in the Kingdom I have no right to sit on.

"Damon, if anyone walks in..."

"They won't." His voice is low. He leans over me to a small console near the right side of the throne. Tapping a few keys, I hear a beep and then a soft click.

"We're locked in," he says. "No one will interrupt us."

His eyes are hooded and dark, and heat gathers in the pit of my stomach. "Why..." I frown, gulping down another breath. "Why do the doors lock from the inside like that?"

"The main ballroom doubles as a safety bunker in case the palace is ever under attack," Damon says with a grin. "So, we're alone. You can relax."

His hands move to my thighs, and he kneels in front of the throne. Slowly, torturously, he slides his palms up under my dress toward my hips. My breath catches. The Prince drags his eyes up to mine as his tongue slides out to lick his lips.

"You're incredible, Dahlia," he breathes. "From the moment I saw you, I needed to have you."

Damon's hands reach my thin, lacy underwear. He teases the outside of the gusset with both his thumbs as his palms stay on my thighs. I whimper, spreading my legs as he touches me. My hands grip the arms of the throne and I bite my lip.

There are so many things wrong with this. Sitting on the throne could have me arrested, for one.

But Damon says we're alone, and he's looking at me like he wants to eat me alive. My breath hitches, and his thumbs drag down across the fabric of my panties again.

"Your Highness..." I sigh, spreading my legs wider. My body is acting of its own accord. His hands grip my thighs and pull me toward the edge of the throne. He grips my legs and pulls them apart, and then flips my dress up to my waist. A low growl rumbles through his chest and I gulp down another breath.

Prince Damon dips his head down and lays a soft kiss on top of my panties. His tongue darts out and licks the crease of my hip. I arch my back. My breath is ragged, my panties are almost soaked through. All I can think of is how much I want him.

*Need* him.

With one hand, he teases the gusset of my underwear again. I tremble, whimpering at the touch. My fingers dig into the throne, its soft velvet crushing under my grip. My nipples pucker under my dress, rubbing against the fabric of my bra. Every sensation is heightened. Every stitch of fabric scratches at my skin, and Damon's hands burn where they touch me.

Prince Damon grins. His fingers slide beneath my panties and when he feels my wetness, he lets out a soft sigh.

"Dahlia, you're so wet," he says gently, dragging his eyes back up to mine. His fingers slide up and down my slit, sending pleasure pulsing through my veins.

My legs are trembling. My fingers grip the throne with all my might as he slides a finger inside me. I gasp, arching my back toward him as his thumb starts circling my clit.

"You didn't tell me you were this wet." His voice is almost chastising, and it's embarrassing how much I like it. He circles my clit with his thumb, dragging another finger in and out of my opening.

I whimper. Somewhere in the back of my mind, I wonder if I'm ruining the velvet seat of the throne.

But it doesn't matter. None of that matters. All that matters is Prince Damon's heady gaze as he watches himself pleasure me, and the feeling of his thick, strong hands fucking me as I sit atop the throne. My underwear is bunched to one side, the fabric adding another layer to the sensation that's becoming almost too much.

I gasp as his thumb presses harder on my bud, but it doesn't last long. In an instant, his lips are on my clit and he's dragging his tongue through my sopping wet slit.

He groans in pleasure, and the fact that he's enjoying this almost sends me over the edge. I've been with so many guys who wouldn't even go near me with their mouth—but not Damon.

Prince Damon hooks his fingers into my panties and rips them down my legs. His hands grip my calves and he lifts my legs up, spreading them wide and staring at me. Splayed out for him, I don't feel embarrassed. I don't feel shy.

All I feel is desire.

"I told you—you're perfect," he sighs. His eyes drag up to mine and I suck a breath in through my teeth. I don't know what to say. My body is pulsing with need and all I can think of is how much I want his lips on me again.

As if he reads my thoughts, Prince Damon hooks my legs over his shoulders and drops his head down. I tangle my fingers into his hair, arching my back and grinding my hips into his face.

He moans, kissing and sucking and licking me until I can't even see straight. His fingers pump inside me again and again as his mouth claims my bud, urging me closer and closer to the edge. I buck and arch and writhe against him, my pastel locks clinging to the velvet back of the throne as my fingers twist into the Prince's hair.

He growls, sending delicious vibrations through my center as his fingers find my most sensitive spot.

"Come for me, Dahlia," the Prince says. "Come on my tongue. I want to taste you." He licks me again, dragging his eyes up to mine. "Come on top of that throne like the dirty girl I know you are."

I whimper, my eyes widening. He licks me again as his fingers thrust in and out of me.

"Come for me, Princess," Damon commands.

"I'm not a pri—" His head drops back down between my legs and he rips the words right out of my mouth. An orgasm crashes through my body as the Prince of Farcliff devours me. I sit half-naked on the throne, my dress bunched around my hips and my underwear lost somewhere below us.

My back arches as heat blazes through me. My legs stiffen and a silent scream spreads my lips. I grip the Prince's hair with both hands and grind his face against my slit as pleasure rocks through my body like never before. I'm a gushing, sopping-wet, trembling *mess*.

Finally, my voice starts to work again, and I let out a moan. The Prince doesn't stop what he's doing. He works his mouth and his hand until he's covered in my honey, moaning in pleasure until I have to push him away.

Everything is too sensitive to touch now.

If I ever thought Damon Farcliff was a play-by-the-rules

kind of guy, I was royally-fucking-*wrong*. He is bad in the best possible way. He's rough, and filthy, and the opposite of clean-cut. He's a savage, and all I know right now is that I want every bit of him.

Damon's lips are swollen and glistening, and his eyes promise more. He leans over my limp, broken body and kisses me. I taste myself on his lips, melting into the throne as he wraps his arms around me once again.

# 10

# DAMON

DESPITE HOW IT MIGHT SEEM, I didn't plan this. But now that we're here and Dahlia is a multicolored, sopping-wet mess on top of the Throne of Farcliff, I'm not mad.

This is definitely the hottest thing I've ever done.

Dahlia reaches between my legs and lets out a soft gasp when she feels my hardness. I'm practically bursting out of my pants.

How else would I be? The woman of my dreams just came for me, on my command, when I held her down on top of the throne. Her legs clamped around my ears and her whole body convulsed as I tasted her orgasm for the first time.

Of course I'm fucking hard.

She glances up at me and then unzips my pants. My cock springs free and Dahlia slides my pants and underwear down. Her delicate fingers wrap around my shaft and a lump forms in my throat.

No, I didn't plan this. Yes, I'm one hundred percent happy with the outcome.

I watch her lips part, and mine open in response. Her tongue swipes across her lower lip, and I do the same to my own. I can still taste her orgasm on my lips, and it makes my cock throb in her hands. She smiles, flicking her eyes up to mine.

I would watch this girl hold my cock in her hand any day of the week.

When she closes her eyes and takes my crown in her mouth, I nearly lose my mind. Her mouth is warm, and wet, and so fucking perfect it makes my head spin. She sucks my cock deep down into her throat and I lean over to catch myself on the back of the throne. My eyes stayed glued on this perfect pixie girl as she works her lips up and down the length of my shaft.

I don't remember the last time I was this turned on. My cock throbs against her lips as she swipes her tongue over the tip. My shaft is glistening with her saliva as she wraps her fingers around the base, squeezing gently as her tongue continues to tease me.

Holy-fucking-Farcliff, Dahlia Raventhal is unreal. My pulse is hammering. My arm is trembling as I hold myself up on the back of the throne. I can't do anything except stare at her mouth as she takes my length inside it once more.

When her eyes dart up to mine and her lips curl into a smile, I almost explode. All I want to do is pull my cock away and cover her in ropes of my cum. Across her plump, pink lips, over her flushed cheeks, into her pastel hair. If she keeps looking at me like that, it won't take long for me to do just that.

I grunt when she pumps her hand up and down my shaft and take a step back.

Her eyebrows shoot up. "You okay?"

"I'm good," I say, gulping down a breath of air. "I'm better than good."

Sweeping my arms around her, I lift her up off the throne

so she's standing in front of me, and I crush my lips against hers. I curl my hand into her hair and pull it back until she gasps, and then I take her lips again. Dahlia rolls her hips toward me and I can't wait any longer.

I reach to the back of her dress and pull down the long zipper that goes down the length of her spine. She pushes my pants off the rest of the way and I kick them away. I kiss her again, more frantically this time. I need her. Dahlia reaches for my shirt, but I put my hand over hers to stop her.

She frowns. "What?"

"Just—leave it on."

"You're self-conscious?" Her hands feel my body through my shirt. "Because let me tell you, Your Highness, you don't have to be. Your body is gorgeous."

I smile, kissing her. I can't tell her that I don't want her to see my scars, my bruises—the evidence of the darkness inside me. As close as I feel to her, I'm not ready to show her that side of me.

We spin around and I fall back onto the throne, sitting in the one seat that will never be mine.

Dahlia's eyes sweep down to my cock, and then she unclasps her bra and lets it fall to the floor. She stands in front of me as I sit on the throne, and for just a moment, we stare at each other.

Her pubic hair is a neatly trimmed, perfectly shaped pastel rainbow, and all I want to do is watch my cock driving in and out of it. Dahlia reaches over to me, sliding her hand over my cock again.

I can't wait any longer. I grab her by the waist and pull her on top of me. Her legs nestle in next to mine, and that multi-colored slit brushes up against my hardened cock.

I shiver in anticipation and my breath catches. My chest is heaving. My hands sink into her thighs.

Dahlia reaches between us and angles my cock against her opening. When she sinks down onto it, we both exhale in unison.

Buried inside her to the hilt, I pause. I can feel her body adjusting to my girth, stretching and pulsing and squeezing me as she lets out a sigh. Dahlia's hands slide over my shoulders and her eyes meet mine. A smile tugs at the corner of her lips, and I know I'm in heaven.

I thrust myself into her—hard. She yelps, squeezing my shoulders and falling into me. Her lips brush my neck as I drive myself inside her again and again. Dahlia catches herself, then, and uses the throne behind me to lift herself up.

Then, I learn just how wild Dahlia Raventhal really is. She bounces on my cock like no one I've ever seen. She hangs off the throne of Farcliff and spears herself with my shaft, gasping and whimpering as our bodies collide. Her tits bounce, her back arches, her legs buck, and we fuck each other hard and fast.

My breath is ragged and my heart is on the verge of exploding in my chest.

Without warning, Dahlia spins around so we're both facing the same way. She leans her back against my chest and grinds herself against me, moaning and letting her head fall against my neck. Her body fits perfectly against mine.

My hands are on her in an instant—one hand across her breast, teasing her nipple. It's hard as a pebble between my fingers and Dahlia moans when I take it between my thumb and forefinger. My other hand drops between her legs, circling her clit. She rewards me with another whimper, rolling her hips against me as my cock sinks even deeper inside her.

Dahlia's hands grip the sides of the throne and I fuck her

mercilessly. She's a rag doll on top of me, bouncing at every thrust as I drive myself inside her. I can't think. I can't speak, I can't do anything except focus on her silken walls gripping my shaft and her perfect, petite body pressed against mine.

I don't want to come yet. This is too good. It's too intense. Too fucking perfect for me to stop.

So, I don't.

Not until I feel her walls contract around my shaft. Not until her body stiffens and her toes curl. Not until both her legs are shaking and she lets out the most gorgeous, perfect scream of ecstasy I've ever heard.

Only then do I let go. With a roar, I empty myself inside her, splashing my cum deep into her as I clutch Dahlia against me.

The only sound in the throne room is the thumping of my heart and the deep, ragged breaths that Dahlia and I take. We sit atop the throne, naked and speechless.

Finally, Dahlia stirs against me and lays a soft kiss against my neck. She lets out a contented sigh and nuzzles her face against my chest.

"I'll be honest, I wasn't expecting that," she says.

"Neither was I," I respond, "but I can't say I hadn't dreamed about it."

She chuckles weakly, and then peels herself off me. Squeezing her legs together she shakes her head. "Is there a bathroom nearby? I've got to clean this mess up," she grins.

"Just out that door, but we'd better get dressed first."

Dahlia leans over to pick up her damp, crumpled-up panties and shakes her head. "You owe me a new pair of undies."

"I will gladly buy—and ruin—as many pairs of underwear as you want."

Dahlia laughs, glancing at me sideways as she slips the

rest of her clothes on. I do the same, and then tap the console to unlock the doors.

"This way," I say, glancing once more at the throne. Apart from one damp spot on the seat, it looks untouched—but I know I'll never look at it the same way again.

Dahlia follows my gaze and a flush creeps over her cheeks. "I can't believe we just did that."

A voice calls out from behind the throne.

"Did what?"

Dahlia and I both freeze, and the blood drains from her face. From a doorway behind the throne, Aunt Malerie steps out of the shadows and into the throne room.

# 11

# DAHLIA

MALERIE FARCLIFF GIVES me the creeps, especially when she looks me up and down two minutes after I had the bejeezus screwed out of me on top of the Throne of Farcliff.

I know I'm blushing. I wouldn't even call it a blush. I'm so red I probably look like I just did an intense sprint in August heat, and also have a sunburn. 'Tomato' doesn't even come close to describing how my face looks right now.

Lady Farcliff steps into the throne room and glances from me, to Damon, and back to me again.

Her eyes are sharp, and her gaze makes me feel naked. Not in the 'I'm at home and I don't care who sees' kind of way. It's a shameful, embarrassed kind of naked feeling that I've never experienced before.

Damon clears his throat. "Aunt Mal," he says. "Nice to see you."

I glance over at him and notice two of the buttons on his shirt have come undone, revealing a sliver of his bare chest. I cringe.

It's painfully obvious what we've just been doing, and if Malerie Farcliff decides to use this bit of gossip to her advantage, I could be in deep, deep trouble. Worse trouble than I'm already in by being involved with Prince Damon. What we just did... that could land me in jail. I could be banished, just like my mother.

Maybe it runs in the family.

Although, something tells me that my mother never did what we just did.

Lady Farcliff takes a step closer to us and my heart beats faster.

"I never thought I'd see the day that another Raventhal was invited to Farcliff Castle." She arches an eyebrow. Her gaze sweeps up and down my body, freezing me on the spot. Even if I wanted to run away, I don't think I could.

I gulp. "The King was very gracious to invite me."

"Gracious," she repeats, swinging her eyes to Damon. "Indeed."

Damon clears his throat. "Is there... Can we help you with anything, Aunt Malerie?"

Lady Farcliff shakes her head so slightly I almost miss the movement. "I was just on my way back in and I heard something... strange. I wanted to make sure no one was in trouble." Her eyes flick to the throne, to that little wet patch on the seat. If the ground opened up at my feet and swallowed me whole right now, I wouldn't be mad. I'd welcome the oblivion with open arms.

Prince Damon, thankfully, notices my discomfort. He puts a hand on my lower back to support me, and the warmth of his skin warms me through the fabric of my dress. With a small bow to his aunt, he gestures to a door on the side wall.

"If you'll excuse us, Aunt, I was just giving Dahlia a tour of the castle. We still have lots of ground to cover."

"Of course," she says, painting a false smile on her face. "Don't let me stop you."

I feel her eyes on my back until the door closes behind us, and I let out a sigh. I turn to Damon and smack his chest with my palm.

"What's that for?" He asks, catching my hand.

"We should never have done that. She *knew*."

"She can't prove anything."

"There's no CCTV in there?"

Damon laughs, catching my chin in his hand. He lays a soft kiss on my lips and wraps his arms around me. "If I wanted to film you, I'd ask you first." His eyes flash. "I mean, if you're into that kind of thing..."

"I'm not," I say, pulling away. My heart is still racing.

This is all wrong. So, so wrong. There is nothing right about this situation.

Not the throne room, not Malerie Farcliff, not me—a Raventhal—being at the castle.

It's *wrong*.

The only thing that felt right was Damon's lips on mine, and his shaft buried deep inside me. That? That was right. That was perfect.

My breath hitches and I squeeze my eyes shut.

If Malerie Farcliff even whispers a word of this to anyone, it would cause a scandal of epic proportions. It could ruin Damon's chances of becoming a well-respected doctor.

It would kill my mother.

"Hey," Damon says softly, stroking my arm. "Come on. It's okay."

"It's not okay, Your Highness," I whisper. "I should never have come here."

"Come on," he says, taking my hand. "The restroom is just down here. We can get cleaned up and then we'll both feel better. Don't worry about Aunt Mal. She's grumpy and easily offended, but she's not dangerous. Her bark is worse than her bite."

I force a smile, but I don't quite believe him. Judging by how my family only said her name in hushed whispers, I suspect that Mal Farcliff's bite is very much as bad as her bark.

Damon leads me to a bathroom. "I'll wait out here," he says. "You go first."

"Thanks." I push the door open and pause, glancing back at him. "Your shirt came unbuttoned, by the way."

"Shit," he says under his breath, looking down at himself. I catch a glimpse of a long, white scar across his chest and I frown, but he buttons his shirt too quickly for me to look more closely. Is that why he didn't want to take his shirt off?

Damon sighs. "I was wondering why she was staring at me like that."

"I think it's obvious what we were doing in there, Damon."

His eyes lift up to mine and a smile flashes across his face. "You called me Damon."

I squeeze my eyes shut and shake my head. "Did you not hear me? She knows what we were doing."

"We're supposed to be two lovebirds dating each other," he says, leaning against the wall. "We're in the honeymoon phase, remember? We should be having sex everywhere and anywhere, multiple times a day." A roguish smile tugs at his lips, and a strand of hair falls across his forehead. My heart skips a beat. Why does he have to be so damn handsome?

Damon reaches over to me and strokes my cheek. "Come on, Dahlia. It's fine. She can't hurt you—no one can. I promise."

"Anyone ever tell you not to make promises you can't keep?"

Damon leans over and kisses my forehead. "I'll be right here. Hurry up, I have to pee."

"Is that how the Prince is supposed to talk to his lover? I thought we were still in the honeymoon phase."

He smiles again, and my heartbeat quickens. Damn my heart and damn him! Why couldn't this be easy? Why did he have to be so perfect for me—and so wrong at the same time?

With a deep breath, I turn away and head into the bathroom. I lock the door behind me and head to the sink, where I splash water on my face to try to calm myself down.

I lean against the marble vanity with my head dropped onto my chest. There are so many emotions warring inside me. My heart and my mind are tugging me in opposite directions.

Heart—and body—toward Damon. Towards the euphoria he creates in me. Towards the mind-blowing orgasms that he gives me.

But my mind holds me back. It reminds me of my upbringing, of the pain of not growing up with my parents, of the danger that my mother always warned me about.

I think of all the questions that remain unanswered, and the feeling in my gut that I shouldn't trust anyone in the Farcliff royal family...

...and I know that my mind has to win.

As much as it kills me, this has to stop. As much as Prince Damon has wriggled his way into my heart, I know it can't go any further than this.

He's not the square, clean-cut guy I thought he was—he's so much more. But I'll never find out exactly what's underneath his proper exterior, because I can't get involved with him.

If only for my mother's sake, I need to keep my distance.

**12**

___

# LADY MALERIE

MALERIE WATCHES Damon and the Raventhal girl disappear through the doorway, and her stomach sours. Her lips turn downward as she shakes her head.

Fifteen years later, she has to deal with yet another Raventhal bitch trying to sink her claws in the royal family. Malerie saw the way Damon looked at Dahlia before their dinner. She saw the way he put his arm protectively around Dahlia when Malerie stared.

He cares about her.

Sweet, stupid Damon.

Wasn't it enough to deal with the death of the Queen? Didn't the Raventhals learn their lesson? Farcliff has had fifteen years of peace, and now it's the same set of problems cropping up all over again.

Well, Malerie won't let it happen again.

Stepping lightly around the throne, she casts an eye over the ornate chair.

Because that's all it is—a chair.

For how many years did she wish she could sit in it? How

87

many times did she resent the fact that her ape of a brother got the title, and the glory, and the power?

Disgusted, Malerie walks across the Great Hall to the opposite side. Her steps echo in the empty room, and she feels so, so alone.

Damon won't get a chance to sit on the throne, either. He's like her—wretched number two. Charlie, the eldest, has always been a king. Everyone knows it—including him. He's been treated like he owns the palace since he was an infant. Gabriel, the youngest of the brothers, has too much of his father in him. Brutish and dark, he'd never make a good ruler.

But Damon? He's different.

He's like Malerie. How she wishes she could teach him how to enjoy his life! She could show him what it means to make the most of a bad hand.

When she reaches the other end of the room, she glances back toward the door through which Damon and the Raventhal girl disappeared. A snarl twists Malerie's lips, and she vows to protect Damon from the girl. Whatever it takes, there won't be another Raventhal slithering around the castle.

# 13

# DAMON

WHEN DAHLIA COMES BACK out of the washroom, I know something has changed. She doesn't say much, but I can feel it.

"I think I'd like to go home now," she says, dragging her eyes up to mine before looking away again.

"You don't want to stay? I was going to show you the rose garden and the royal beehive. It produces all the honey in Farcliff, right here on the castle grounds. My aunt brought the bees back from Yemen when I was a kid." I'm blabbing, but I don't care. I'll say anything to get her to stay.

"I'm allergic to bees and I don't have my EpiPen," Dahlia blurts out.

I chuckle, confused. "Okay, no beehive, then. Just a walk around the grounds?"

Dahlia shifts her weight from foot to foot. With a deep breath, she lifts her eyes up to mine again. "Look, Damon. Tonight was incredible. I really like you—I do..." She pauses.

"Sounds like there's a 'but' in there." I try to keep my voice neutral, but it trembles ever so slightly on the last word.

"...but I don't think it's a good idea for us to get involved.

Your family still hates mine, and neither of us really know what happened between them."

"We are not our parents, Dahlia. We're allowed to do what we want."

"I know. I just..." She takes a deep breath. "I just can't. I'm sorry." She shakes her head, and my heart sinks.

We walk in silence back the way we came, through the double doors at the castle entrance and toward the waiting car.

Dahlia leaves the palace grounds without another word.

Suddenly, I feel cold. My throat is scratchy as I watch the car drive away, hoping that she'll change her mind. I watch the taillights disappear through the tall gates, standing on the castle steps like a fool. Then, I turn back to the castle with a slump in my shoulders.

Trudging back to my chambers, I push the door open and sigh. My books are laid out ready for me on my desk, but I just don't have the energy to study right now.

I don't have the energy to do anything except re-live every second of this evening over and over again.

Dahlia, the proper lady at a royal dinner party, followed by Dahlia, the decidedly *un*-proper lady splayed out on the Throne of Farcliff for me. I can still see her lips falling open in a silent scream when she came, and I can feel her hands twisting into my hair. I can taste her skin. Her honey. Her kiss.

But she's gone.

I stare at my desk full of notebooks and assignments, and I sigh. Is this really what I want?

My father has been supportive of me giving up my royal duties to pursue medical school. I'm not the eldest, so it's not like I have responsibilities as the heir to the throne. For the most part, I've done well. I'll be starting my residency at

Farcliff General Hospital in September, and I just have a round of exams to get through before then.

I should be studying.

But my thoughts keep circling back to Dahlia—to the way that she said goodbye. I stare at my desk, at my laptop, at my books, and my arms hang limply at my sides.

I know this feeling. I call it the Darkness. The Darkness starts in the depths of my heart, usually on nights like tonight. When something throws me off emotionally, or physically, or mentally, I can feel it creeping into the corners of my soul. Before too long, it'll consume me whole.

When I was younger, it was overwhelming. It started right after my mother died in her bed. After I saw her—cold and rigid, her eyes glassy as they stared up at the ceiling—the Darkness started.

When I saw the cup of tea that I'd brought her the night before, spilled on its side on the thick carpet below her bed, I knew I would never be the same.

I'd stay in my own bed for days, unable to move or speak or do anything except lay there and wait for the feeling to go away. The Darkness was like a crushing physical weight sitting in the center of my chest.

As I got older, I learned to see the warning signs. Sometimes, it was like a pendulum. If I felt too happy about something, it was only a matter of time before the pendulum swung the other way. The higher the highs, the lower the lows.

Dinner with Dahlia was a high. Sex with Dahlia was definitely a fucking high. It was stratospheric. Having her naked in my arms was like nothing I'd ever felt before.

Watching her drive away without looking back? That was a low.

Nowadays, I can usually stop the Darkness from taking

over. Over the years, I've gotten better at keeping it at bay. The tingling in my fingertips, the loss of feeling in my lips. The thoughts circling in my mind like sharks.

It all leads down the same road—to the deep, dark abyss of my own soul.

I can usually stop that from happening. Sometimes I throw myself into my studies. Sometimes I work out. Sometimes I drink.

But when things are bad, the only thing that keeps the Darkness at bay is pain.

Tonight, it's bad.

I throw open my bedroom door and pull on a jacket. It's the end of March, and Farcliff is still cold. It won't be summer for another few months.

I zip my jacket up to my chin and stuff my hands in my pockets. I cross a few people in the castle hallways on my way to the garages, but no one says a word to me.

Not that I'd answer. There's only one thing on my mind right now. I need to feel something. I need to get Dahlia out of my head. I need to keep the Darkness from taking over.

When I make it to my car, my hands are trembling, and it isn't because of the cold. It's taking all my energy to keep my body together, as if some invisible force is trying to tear my body to pieces. The Darkness is overwhelming my heart and starting to cloud my vision. I put the car in gear and drive off the castle grounds. My heart thumps so hard it hurts.

My jaw clenches and my teeth grind together as I make my way through the tree-lined, well-kept streets of Farcliff toward the other half of the Kingdom. Toward Grimdale.

Grimdale is the only place where I can get what I need right now. I take my car down the familiar streets as the buildings get more run-down and the trees grow fewer. The transition from Farcliff to Grimdale is almost instantaneous.

In Farcliff, the streetlights are bright, the sidewalks are swept clean, the storefronts are happy and prosperous. Grimdale, on the other hand, is... Well, it's grim. It's grey, the paint is peeling everywhere, the streetlights flicker ominously. Men with hoods pulled up over their heads wander the streets, ducking their faces away from my headlights.

I taste blood in my mouth as I make the final turn and park my car behind a run-down warehouse. When I stop the engine, I can already hear the dull thumping of fists against flesh.

My eyes are cloudy and my hands shake as I secure my wallet and phone in the glove compartment. I get out, casting a glance toward the huge warehouse. I lock my car.

My feet crunch on gravel as I make my way to the building. It's dark—the only light here comes from underneath the warehouse door. Muffled shouts sound from the other side of the door. I close my eyes and gather my courage.

I have to do this. I have to be here.

I push the warehouse door open.

Inside, the light is low and the air is heavy. On the far end of the empty room is a makeshift boxing ring. Bloodthirsty gamblers scream out as two men beat themselves to a pulp inside the ropes. One fighter—a light-haired man—has a split lip and his eye is swollen shut. It's not stopping his flurry of punches from landing on his opponent's midsection, though. The other man's eyes roll back. Blood pours from a cut above his eye.

The knockout punch comes right as I step up to the edge of the ring. The blond man stands over his unconscious opponent, arms hanging by his side and his lip curled into an ugly snarl. He lets out a roar that sends a tremor through my body.

The spectators salivate, screaming wordlessly at the fighters.

I jump when a heavy hand lands on my shoulder.

"Prince," Nigel says to me with a grin. "Haven't seen you in a while."

I grunt and Nigel's eyes flash.

"Over here." He leads me away from the main ring and through a doorway on the other side of the warehouse. We end up in a small, dark room with no windows. It has no furniture, and the floor has dark, rust-colored stains all over it.

Blood—some of it mine.

I open and close my fists and turn toward Nigel.

He grins. "The usual?"

I nod, pulling out a wad of cash. "Yeah. Not the face."

"Wouldn't dream of it. Ravi!" Nigel calls through the door, and a mammoth of a man steps through. His forehead protrudes over his eyes and he lets out a low growl. Nigel nods to me. "This man wants a Farcliff Royalty special. Don't touch his pretty, princely face."

Ravi grunts, and a small part of me regrets coming here. It's only a small part of me, though, and when Ravi lands his first punch to my ribs, my regret is replaced with pain.

Beautiful, addictive, blinding pain.

I let out a laugh, spreading my arms as Ravi punches me again, and again, and again. Agony explodes through my abdomen as I'm flung from one side to the other. I stumble, keeping my footing, and Ravi connects with my ribs again.

They crack, and white-hot pain shoots through me. My feet wobble and I collapse onto one knee.

"Stop," Nigel says as Ravi steps closer to me. The big Neanderthal pauses, and I scrape myself off the floor and back to my feet. "Enough?" Nigel asks.

I shake my head, wheezing. "I'm here to get my money's worth."

The darkness in my soul poisons my veins. It turns my heart black and clouds my thoughts as the big man punches me over, and over, and over again. Every hit sends suffering shooting through me, and it feeds the broken part of me that thrives on hurt. My ribs crack, my organs scream.

I don't hit back. I don't fight. I just feed off it.

As Ravi hits me and Nigel watches, I think of Dahlia. I think of her naked body, and how I know I won't get to touch it again. Her hair, her spirit, her carefree laugh. I don't deserve her. There's a part of me that's rotten, and the only way to keep it down is to beat it out of me.

I know she said goodbye forever. I know she won't come back to the castle. I know that I'll probably never love a woman who loves me back. How could I? Who could love someone who does this to themselves? Who could love someone whose darkness overwhelms them like mine does?

I lean into the pain and laugh as I'm pummeled. I hurt... but at least I'm feeling something. I'll wake up bruised and battered tomorrow. It'll hurt to walk and move and breathe... but I'll wake up. I'll get up. I'll move.

Ravi beats me until the pain becomes too much and I pass out. I know that Nigel will drag me to another room, where I'll wake up on a cheap cot with ice on my bruises.

It's the royal treatment. The Prince Damon special. The only cure for the darkness in my heart.

# 14

# DAHLIA

I RESIST the urge to glance back through the rear windshield of the royal car as we drive away from the castle. I can't feel the Prince's eyes following me, just like I can feel where his hands marked me, where his tongue devoured me.

But Prince Damon isn't enough to make me stay. I saw the way Lady Malerie was looking at me, and I know I wasn't welcome at the palace.

Ever since I was a small child, I've been told that Farcliff—especially Farcliff Castle—is a dangerous place. I was sequestered far, far away from the Kingdom, living in a little forest town deep in the Rocky Mountains. I was safe there.

My mother has always insisted that the Farcliff royal family was dangerous.

After tonight, I don't know what to think.

I've met Prince Charlie, the eldest son and heir to the throne. He's dating my roommate and best friend, Elle. I think he has her best interests at heart.

Prince Damon seems like a good guy—and not in the 'perfect prince who gives up his royal privilege to pursue medical school' kind of way. He seems like a genuinely good person.

But the rest of them? I don't know.

Massaging my temples, I try to shake loose the fears and worries that seem to gather just behind my eyes. A pulsing headache is starting to form.

Lulled by the gentle movement of the car, I close my eyes. I can still smell Prince Damon's cologne, and I sigh.

This is what always happens with my love life. If I happen to meet someone that I like for more than one night—which is rare—something always comes between us. In this case, our families.

As much as I'd love to be with him, I just can't bring myself to betray my mother's trust like that. She's already hurt herself once this week. What would happen if she found out about tonight? I can't risk my mother's safety for my own love life.

I know I can't be with him.

So, why do my thoughts keep drifting to what happened in the throne room? Why am I itching to ask the driver to turn around and take me back to the castle? Why is it so difficult to say goodbye to the Prince?

I know what the royal family is like. I know what they did to my mother—exiled her and ruined our family name—and I know they wouldn't hesitate to do the same to me. Dinner tonight went well, all things considered, but it has to end there.

I wasn't at the castle to redeem my family name, and I wasn't there to fall in love with Prince Damon. I was there for Elle.

The Farcliff royal family is dangerous. They're power-hungry, single-minded people who are used to being at the top of the food chain.

... Right?

Isn't that what I was always told? Isn't that what my mother taught me?

And who am I? I'm just the daughter of a woman who was thrown out of the Kingdom almost fifteen years ago. I'm a nobody.

No, I'm not a nobody. I'm a Raventhal, and that's even worse than being nobody.

With a deep, shaking breath, I try to ease the tightness between my shoulders. Reaching back into my hair, I pull out the thousand and one hairpins that are keeping my mane under control. When I run my fingers through my locks, I breathe a sigh of relief.

The castle is behind me, and I don't need to see Prince Damon or the King at all anymore.

When I get home, I thank the driver and slip back inside my old house. I hear Elle shuffling around, and I know she wants to hear about my evening.

Her relationship hinges on the King's opinion of me, and whether we fooled him into believing that Prince Damon and I are an item. Of course she wants to know how it went.

But right now, I don't have the energy to talk to her about it. I don't want to tell her what happened in the throne room. Not that Elle would mind—she's used to my sexcapades—but this... It's different.

What happened between Damon and me is private. It's my little secret—one that I'll keep locked in a corner of my heart for the rest of my life. It would feel wrong to tell Elle.

Crawling under my blankets, I huddle in a tight ball and try to move on from this evening. I went to the palace to help Elle, but I don't know that I'd have the heart to do it over.

I don't think I'd be able to walk away from Prince Damon again.

But walk away, I must. My loyalty has to be to my family. I can't turn my back on them for the sake of mind-melting orgasms. I've never been a selfish person before, and I can't become one now.

This is the way it has to be. Or at least, that's what I keep telling myself.

Beneath it all, there's a teasing heat that curls at the pit of my stomach. When Prince Damon looked at me with his bright, blue eyes, it made me question my past, and my future.

It made me wonder if maybe my mother was wrong about the Farcliff family. All this talk about curses and danger—how much of it is true?

Then, I shake my head and bring the blankets up to my chin. I focus on my breath, and I try to fall asleep.



Elle is up and awake, as usual. She always wakes up before dawn to go to rowing practice every day with the Farcliff University crew team, so she's guaranteed to be up when I wake.

I pour myself a mug of coffee and nod. "It was good!" My voice goes up a couple octaves.

"Did the King buy it?"

"Buy what?"

"That you were dating Prince Damon." Elle frowns, grinning in confusion. "You know, the whole reason you went to the dinner in the first place?"

"Oh, right. Yeah, I think so." I sip my coffee and avoid her eye.

Elle's eyebrows draw together. I know she's worried about

her relationship with Prince Charlie, but right now I just don't have the energy to think about it. My best friend keeps looking at me and I force a smile. She's used to seeing me bubbly and carefree, and her forehead is creased with concern.

"Did you see much of the castle?" She takes a seat next to me at the kitchen table.

*I saw some of it.*

I force a grin. "Not as much as you did during your first romp through the castle."

"It was definitely a romp," Elle laughs. She shakes her head. "But seriously, was everything okay?"

With a deep breath, I try to smile wider. "It was fine. The King seemed fairly uninterested in me. Prince Charlie seemed happy. I think he really likes you."

She blushes and her eyes get a faraway look. Diverting the conversation to her secret boyfriend works like a charm, and she doesn't ask me too much else about the castle—or about Prince Damon.

It's a great trick. If you don't want to talk about something, just get the other person to talk about themselves. Conversation tricks 101—works especially well with men.

Except, not with Prince Damon.

Conversation with him is deeper. I close my eyes and start thinking of him again. His broad, strong hands sinking into my hips. His chest, his shoulders, the way his hair fell across his forehead. His tongue, lapping me up as I lay splayed out in front of him.

He's gorgeous.

A week ago, I wouldn't have given anything a second thought. I believed everything my mother had told me about the Farcliff royal family, and I'd grown up in blissful ignorance surrounded by the forest, birds, and my three lovely aunts. I believed that Farcliff was dangerous, and that the royal family wanted to cause us harm.

But now, I'm not so sure.

Elle thankfully leaves for class, and I'm left alone. I mope around my house and finally pull myself together for class. My phone dings—a message from a guy I was seeing last week. It just says 'Hey'.

How original.

I don't want to text this guy. Nothing about him was interesting. Nothing about him was exciting. Even his message is boring.

He's not Damon Farcliff.

Yet, I know in my heart of hearts that I have to keep my distance from Prince Damon. If only for my mother, or for my own peace of mind.

I unlock my phone, and instead of answering the text, I find Damon's number. My fingers hover over the name and I take a deep breath.

With a couple taps, I delete his phone number and erase the few texts we've sent each other. I wipe any memory of him off my phone—there isn't much, but there's enough.

I bite my lip and let out a heavy sigh. I need to stay away from the castle and the entire royal family.

Staying away means no more Prince Damon. No more dinners. No more heat in the pit of my stomach and definitely no orgasms on the Throne of Farcliff.

# 15

# DAMON

WHEN I WAKE UP, my head isn't exactly clear, but at least it's empty. The blankets on my small cot are scratchy and they smell stale. I push myself up to a seated position and glance around the room. My body screams in pain. The ceiling has a bit water stain, and the walls are bare concrete.

There's a bottle of water on the side table, and the sight of it makes me realize how dry my mouth feels. I reach for the water, wincing as pain flashes through my ribs. I crack the bottle open and drink half of it in one gulp. It's lukewarm and it tastes like plastic, but I groan in satisfaction.

I stand up gingerly, every movement sending more daggers of pain stabbing through my chest. I lift my shirt up and look at my ribs. They're mottled blue and purple— almost black in places. My left hip is sore, and when I move, it feels like all my bones and joints are out of whack.

But when I bring my hands up to my face, it feels exactly as it did yesterday. No cuts, no swelling, no bruises.

I leave some money on the side table as a tip. It helps keep people quiet when they're well paid. Gathering my car keys, I make my way outside.

When I walk out into the main room, the makeshift boxing ring has disappeared. The warehouse is empty. Everyone is gone. The only evidence of last night's fights is a couple of faded blood splatters on the wall. Dragging my feet over to the exit, I push it open and wince.

The sunlight needles my eyes and I bring a forearm up to shield my face. Lifting my arm up sends a jolt of pain through my side and I gasp. I shuffle to the driver's side door and get in, fumbling with the center console to get my sunglasses. When I have them on, I breathe a sigh of relief.

My mind feels blank—exactly how I want it. The spiraling, chaotic thoughts that brought me here last night are gone.

In that moment, alone in my car, I think of Dahlia again. I think of her body, boneless and broken on top of me when we fucked on the Throne of Farcliff. I think of her smile, her voice, her smell.

It doesn't hurt like it did last night. Even knowing that I probably won't see her again doesn't make me sad.

I don't feel anything.

If a hint of a feeling starts to thread its way through my heart, all I have to do is move my body a fraction of an inch and the agony clears my head again.

She's gone.

I find my phone in the glove compartment and turn it on. I find Dahlia's number and stare at it for a minute or two. Then, with a sigh, I lock my phone and put it away.

If she wants to call me, she can call me. I'm not going to chase after a woman. It's not what a Prince does.

I make my way home and I lock myself in my bedroom. I shower, I change, and I sit down in front of my textbooks to study.

. . .

DAHLIA DOESN'T CALL—NOT for months. Even at the Spring Regatta, where Elle competes and the entire royal family is there to watch, Dahlia isn't anywhere to be seen. I think I catch a glimpse of someone in a furry pink jacket, but I'm whisked away before I can be sure it's her.

In my heart, though, I know it's her. Who else would wear something like that?

Instead of pining over her, I do what I've always done—I throw myself into my studies. I don't go out, I don't party, or drink, or date. I forget about Dahlia.

Well, forget is the wrong word. I think about her all the time, and it drives me crazy. How could someone have such an effect on me after just a couple of days?

But she never calls me back, and my pride stops me from reaching out to her. I just let it go.

It was fun, we fucked, and that was it. We weren't even dating for real—we were just helping Charlie out.

Now, it's over.


THANKFULLY, come autumn, my medical residency starts at the Farcliff General Hospital, and I don't have time to think about much else. I don't need Ravi to beat me up anymore, because I'm so tired I can't think of anything except my studies. My rotations are four weeks long, each in different departments at the hospital. I put my hand up for the night shift more often than any other person.

My doubts about medical school start to fade away as I spend more and more time at the hospital. My attending physician, Dr. Adler, is a no-nonsense woman with sharp eyes and a sharper tongue.

I'm exhausted most of the time.

In the dead of night, though, when my eyes are heavy and I drift in the space between wakefulness and sleep, I think of Dahlia. She creeps into my dreams uninvited. In a hidden corner of my heart, where only the truth can live, I know that I have to see her again.

## 16

## DAHLIA

THE MONTHS that I spend apart from Prince Damon feel like living in perpetual night. He's the sun, and I know he's there —I just can't see him. There's a world between us. I spend my days in darkness, without his warmth, or light, or his life-giving energy.

I finish off my junior year at Farcliff University and head down to California, where my parents have been living. It's been three months since my mother had her fall and broke her hip, and now she's back on her feet again. My parents wrap me in a warm hug when I arrive and I paint a smile on my face.

College is good, I tell them. Elle is doing well, I say.

I don't mention Prince Damon, for obvious reasons.

I bring them a jar of coveted Farcliff honey, which they haven't tasted since their exile. My father smiles wide and plants a kiss on my cheek. My mother turns her nose up, and says that she thinks my bee allergy was caused by the honeybees at the royal hives.

When I'm sure that my mother is fine, and I've convinced

myself that breaking it off with the Prince was the right decision, I go home to my aunts in Colorado. After a month with my aunts, listening to the crickets in the evening and the birds in the morning, I feel like I'm going to explode.

I'm restless.

I toss and turn in my bed every night, wondering what it would feel like to have the weight of Damon's arm across my body. I can't stop thinking about him—wondering, wishing, hoping.

Trying to forget.

Finally, halfway through the summer, I head back to Farcliff. Elle is pregnant with Prince Charlie's baby—but I'll let her tell that story for herself. I tell my aunts that she needs my help.

Mostly, though, I'm just too far away from Damon—not that I'd ever admit that to anyone.


In September, classes start again, and I have more than enough going on to keep myself distracted. I get an internship at one of Farcliff University's labs, so I'm busy with school, work, and research.

My bed stays cold and empty, because I can't bring myself to replace the Prince. I'll eventually go back to my old ways, I tell myself. I'll sleep with someone else, and I'll get over the Prince—just not tonight.

Or the next night.

Or the next.

When I try to flirt with someone, I lose interest. When I try to bring myself to date, it feels wrong. I even stopped taking my birth control. My prescription ran out, and I didn't see the point in getting another. If I'm not having sex, why would I?

. . .

ONE EVENING IN MID-SEPTEMBER, Elle's baby kicks. We smile and squeal in excitement together. Elle, heartbroken as she is over Prince Charlie, is happy.

She glances at me. "I haven't heard any marathon sex sessions in a while. You okay?"

"Yeah," I say, giving her a tight smile. "Just a dry spell, I guess."

I can see it in her face that she doesn't believe me, but I can't tell her about Prince Damon now—not after her secret relationship with Prince Charlie fell apart.

Then, we flick on the television and find out Charlie's wedding is set for the first of November. Elle's heart breaks all over again, and I push thoughts of Prince Charlie's brother into the back corner of my mind—hidden from everybody, including myself.

The Princes of Farcliff are officially dead to us.

How is it that months can drag on and on, and yet at the same time, they go by in a flash?

Life just marches onward, and I'm carried along by its current. In a way, it feels like I'm watching life happen to everyone around me. Elle's baby bump grows, and grows, and grows. She pulls herself together and works harder than I've ever seen her work and gets ready to be a mother.

I'm proud of her.

But me? What do I do?

I go to school and study. I work at the lab. I watch Elle become a woman.

I pine after a man that I knew for a week, nearly eight months ago.

I'm adrift, aimless, and maybe a little pathetic. Anton Chekhov once said: *When a person is born, he can embark on only one of three roads of life: if you go right, the wolves will eat you; if you go left, you'll eat the wolves; if you go straight, you'll eat yourself.*

I guess this is what it feels like to eat myself.

In those months, I realize that there is no curse. There's just me—my hopes, my fears, my strengths and everything else inside me that holds me back. No, there's no all-knowing curse that drags my life down at every turn. I do that to myself.

Aunt Theresa was right—I'm just clumsy.

WHEN PRINCE CHARLIE proposes to Elle in November, my heart nearly explodes of happiness for her. It's the first time in a long time that I feel anything. The King abdicates, and we find out the Queen was murdered. How, exactly, isn't clear yet, but there's evidence of foul play.

My mother was right all those years ago. My heart skips at the thought—maybe this is it! Maybe this is the moment that the Raventhals are redeemed! Maybe... I shake my head before I can think of the Prince too deeply.

I call my mother as soon as I hear the news, and all she does is sigh in response. My heart sinks.

Farcliff Kingdom falls into complete panic. Charlie is named King, which means Elle will become the new Queen of Farcliff. After the drama of Charlie's proposal dies down—which is her story to tell—Elle comes back to our little old house on the edge of Grimdale and asks me to move to the castle with her.

She lowers herself down onto our old couch, her pregnant stomach looking like it's ready to pop at any moment.

She's glowing, and not just in the pregnancy kind of way. She looks so happy it's impossible not to smile with her.

"There's more than enough room for you, Dahlia. Now that the King has abdicated, you shouldn't feel uncomfortable at the castle. Things are different, now."

I suck in a breath and look away. It's hard to see her like this—so happy and in love—when I still feel uneasy. I'm happy for her, of course, but it's hard to shake feelings that I've carried with me my whole life. Besides, how would I face Damon? Has he moved on? Am I just supposed to move into the same building as him and we pick up where we left off?

*Ha! As if!*

"I think I'd rather stay here," I say, motioning to our dilapidated house. "All my stuff is here."

"We can move your stuff, Dahl," Elle smiles. "It would take a couple hours at most. I can get some men from the castle to help."

I shake my head. "I can't. I'm sorry."

"Are you still worried about the royal family?"

"A little," I admit.

"Even though I'm marrying one of them?"

"Charlie's different."

Elle sighs. "I think the King was a bad apple, Dahlia. You don't have to be scared of the royal family anymore. Invite your parents back to Farcliff."

I wring my hands and bite my lip. "I'll ask them," I finally say. I already know how my mother feels—she's not in any rush to come back here.

Still, something stirs in my chest—something I haven't felt in a long time. My thoughts bounce between Prince Damon, my mother and father, and Elle at the castle with Charlie.

To their baby...

...and I feel hope.

*What if...*

Elle takes a seat beside me on the couch in our living room—well, I guess it's just *my* living room now—and she looks around the house with a faraway look in her eyes. I can tell what she's doing. She's saying goodbye to this place—where we've had so many good times and bad times together. Where we became adults together.

Where she lived when she fell in love.

And me?

Well, I'm still here. Still afraid of the castle. Still torn between my duty to my family and my desire to be my own person. Still thinking of my evening sitting on the Throne of Farcliff.

Elle glances at me. "What about Damon?"

My spine stiffens. "What about him?"

"He'd like to see you at the castle."

"Would he?" I scoff. I shake my head. "I don't think so."

"Why not?"

"Well, for one, I'm still a Raventhal. Just because my mother was right about the Queen's death, doesn't mean they'll welcome us back with open arms."

"Of course they will, Dahlia," Elle smiles. "Charlie said so himself. No one resents the Raventhals anymore."

"The King does. His sister does. The investigation is still ongoing. How do we know who we can trust at the castle and who we can't?"

*Excuses, excuses, excuses.* That's all I hear coming out of my own mouth, when what's really holding me back is the thought of facing Damon again.

"The King isn't the King anymore," Elle says gently. "Charlie is King, now, and he doesn't hold it against you. He loves you—just like I do."

I smile sadly and take a deep breath. "I don't know how to explain it, Elle... It just makes me uneasy to go to the castle."

"Even now?"

"Even now."

Elle sighs. "Okay. Well, at least be my maid of honor."

I turn to look at her and a smile tugs at my lips. "Really?"

"Really. I wouldn't want anyone else at my side. The wedding is in two weeks, and I don't want to do it without you."

My face breaks into a smile and I lean on Elle's shoulder. She has one hand on her pregnant stomach, and she hooks the other arm around my back.

"I can't believe you're getting married so soon."

"Got to do it before this little monster comes out," she says. I can hear the grin in her voice. I watch her rub her hand over her belly. "So, that's a yes?" She asks.

"Of course it's a yes," I laugh. "I'll go to the castle for your wedding, at least, even if I don't want to move there."

Elle squeezes my shoulder. "Deal. Once the investigation is over, will you reconsider coming to the castle? I would love to have a familiar face there."

I tuck a strand of hair behind my ear and nod, smiling. "I'll think about it."

"Good."

Elle heaves herself up to her feet and lets out a breath. "I'm looking forward to getting this baby out, I can tell you that much."

"Can't wait to meet him." I smile.

She gives me a hug and walks toward the front door. There are security guards waiting outside the door, and two more men waiting by a black sedan with tinted windows. Elle lets one of the security guards help her in and I watch from the front porch, giving her one last wave as my best friend is driven back to the castle by her entourage.

To her new home.

I turn back to my old house with a sigh. Things have changed—I know they have. I should face the castle, face my fears, and face the Prince.

Prince Damon did something to me in that throne room, and it scares me. I'm not the type of person who drops everything for a man I don't know, or stays hung up on someone for months. I'm not the type of person who gets thrown off so easily.

Damon throws me off. Even when he doesn't know he's doing it—when I haven't seen him in months—he still makes my head spin.

I scoff, shaking my head. This year has been so turbulent that I need a break just to make sense of it all.

I don't want to move to the castle. I don't want to be that close to him, because it strips me of all my defenses and makes me feel like I don't know myself anymore.

But when I enter my house again, looking around at the peeling paint and dust bunnies in the corners, I let out a deep breath and bring my fingers to the bridge of my nose.

The King abdicated, and there's a royal inquest into the former Queen's death. All the questions I have about the past, about my mother, about my childhood—they could all be answered.

This changes *everything*.

There it is again—hope. Fickle, unreliable, heartbreaking hope.

Prince Damon and I? We might have a chance. Maybe I *could* see him again, and not be scared of the consequences.

The thought makes my heart thump and my stomach

clench. I run my fingers through my hair put a hand to my chest.

Elle's wedding is in two weeks, which means in two weeks, I'll see Damon again. I'll be in the same room as him. I'll smell him, and watch him, and maybe even touch him.

In two weeks, I'll find out if he still thinks about me the same way I think about him.

# 17

# DAMON

I straighten my tie and take a deep breath. The past month has been difficult. Charlie discovered that our father, the King, had our mother murdered fifteen years ago, and I've been having a tough time getting past it. I've gone to see Nigel at the warehouse half a dozen times since I found out.

Anyone would have a hard time with that, but I have other demons to deal with. All my fears are coming to fruition. Maybe my memories of that night are true after all.

Maybe it really was my fault.

A knock on my door makes me turn my head. "Come in," I call out.

My youngest brother, Gabriel, walks in. His dark, chocolate-brown hair is disheveled, and his tie is crooked. His eyes are hazy, as if he's been drinking already.

I sigh. "Hey, Gabe."

"How you doin'?" He slurs his words a bit and flops down onto the nearest chair. Gabe isn't a bad guy—he's just angry. While I deal with my anger in private, and Charlie takes it out on the punching bags, Gabe hasn't quite found a way to release it yet. He's just turned nineteen, and it looks like he's at the start of one long, downward spiral.

I know exactly how that feels, but I don't know how to help him.

I shrug. "I'm fine. Just going to try to get through today with a smile on my face."

"Yeah." Gabe rests his head on his fist and lets out a sigh. He was just a kid when our mother was killed. He barely remembers her, and I think that hurts him more than anything else. As he's gotten older, he's talked about it less and less.

"You okay?" I ask, heading to the mini fridge and pulling out two beers. Gabe accepts one of them with a nod.

"Not really. I get why Charlie has to get married—he's going to be crowned soon, and he needs a wife. His girlfriend is pregnant, so they want to get married before the baby comes. I get that, I really do. It's just..."

"...it's quick."

"Yeah," Gabe sighs. "We just found out all this shit about Father, and now we're supposed to turn around and celebrate?"

"I think that's why he's just having a small ceremony, with only close friends and family."

"I know, but it just feels wrong. How am I supposed to be happy for him when I know that my mom was murdered by my fucking father?" A vein in his neck pulses.

"I know." More than I can say to him, *I know*. I fucking know how he feels. It's simmering just below the surface in all three of us.

"Do you know, though? You seem to be doing all right."

"Gabe..."

"What?" His voice has an edge to it that wasn't there a second ago.

I take a deep breath. "All I'm saying is—let's just make it through today and be happy for Charlie. The investigation is ongoing, so we can deal with the fallout after. Maybe it's a good thing we have this wedding right now. It's a distraction from all the other shit going on."

Gabe grunts in response. It kills me that he feels like this, but there's nothing I can do about it. We sip our drinks in silence, and then I push myself up to my feet.

"We should get down there."

My brother lets out a heavy sigh and follows me down to the Great Hall. I've avoided this room ever since Dahlia was in here with me. Every time I see the throne, I think of what happened on top of it.

They're not bad memories—I just wish they weren't just memories. I wish they were a daily occurrence, and not a flash in my past.

The ceremony will start any minute, and I find Charlie near the throne. I clap him on the shoulder.

"Congratulations, brother," I say.

"Thanks, Damon." His face is lined with tiredness—just like Gabriel's face and my own. Just like everyone's face has been lined since we found out the news about our father.

Unlike Gabe and me, Charlie's eyes are bright with happiness.

I take my spot beside him, and Gabe takes his place beside me. Gabe wavers on his feet a little, but stays standing. I just hope he makes it through the ceremony without passing out or vomiting. There's definitely a beast inside my little brother, and I don't want him to let it out today.

Music sounds from behind us, and the ceremony begins. There aren't many people in attendance—maybe thirty, total. Our family, our closest friends, and the people we know we can trust. No press, no journalists, no outsiders.

The doors at the end of the room open and my breath catches in my throat.

*Dahlia.*

I knew there was a good chance she'd be here. A part of me hoped she would. A part of me never wanted to see her again, just to avoid the bottomless feeling I get in my stomach whenever she's around.

But she's here, and she's perfect. She's dressed in a blushing, pink dress that swirls around her feet as she walks up the aisle. Her hair is platinum blonde now, curled into soft waves that fall to her mid-back. The ends are dyed bright, neon pink.

I want her.

Any anger that I had over her rejection—any resentment that existed in my heart—it's gone. As soon as she steps into the Great Hall, I know I want her again.

*Need* her again.

If I had my way, everyone else in this room would disappear and I'd sit Dahlia on the throne once more, spread those perfect legs wide and make her mine until the only word on her lips was my name.

But that doesn't happen. Instead, Dahlia's eyes lift up to mine and her cheeks blush to match her dress. She's carrying a small bouquet of flowers. As she holds my gaze, Dahlia stumbles and lets out a soft swear word.

I grin.

She catches herself and, with a breath, makes her way to the other side of the dais, opposite where my brothers and I are waiting. As Dahlia takes her position, I notice that the back of her dress plunges down to reveal her milky white back. My fingers itch to feel her skin, to tease their way up her vertebrae and tangle themselves into her hair.

My cock throbs.

I don't hear any of the ceremony. I'm sure it's beautiful, but all I hear is the thumping of my heart in my ears. All I see is a blur, punctuated by the many glances I steal toward Dahlia.

She does the same, and hope blooms inside me. She feels the same way I do—I know she does. What if this whole mess with my father turns out to be a good thing? What if her hesitation to come to the castle goes away? What if we have another chance at this?

I clap at all the right times, and I take pictures when I'm supposed to. The wedding ceremony is quick and—I'm told later—very moving. But the only thing that moves me right now is a short pixie-girl that I want to make my own.

Finally, after an eternity, the ceremony ends and we're led to one of the large reception rooms in the castle. Dahlia stands near the wall, and it only takes a couple of seconds for her eyes to find mine. From across the room, we stare at each other.

There are a thousand words in that gaze. A million things we haven't said to each other—and don't need to speak out loud.

My body responds by burning hotter. My cock throbs. I drop my gaze to her body, and suddenly my feet are carrying me toward her. Her cheeks flush. My mouth waters. Her hands tremble slightly, until she clasps them together. Her tongue slides out to swipe her lower lip.

I *need* her.

We stand a foot apart, and it takes every ounce of my willpower to stop from throwing her over my shoulder and carrying her to the closest private room.

After a moment, she sucks in a breath. "Hey."

"Hey," I respond. I gulp past a lump in my throat. My palms are sweating. "You look great. And I don't mean that as flattery. It's the truth. So, you know—tell Dostoyevsky the two aren't mutually exclusive."

"Thanks," she laughs. "You clean up all right, too."

I take a deep breath. Gathering all my courage, I nod to the door. "You want to go somewhere quiet to talk?"

Her eyes darken ever so slightly, and a smile tugs at her lips. "Yeah, I do."

# 18

# DAHLIA

EVEN THOUGH I told myself that I'd be strong, that I wouldn't let myself be alone with Prince Damon, that I'd keep my distance... the instant I saw him, I knew I was destined to fail.

How can I resist, when he's the definition of irresistible?

His hand drifts to the small of my back as he leads me through a side door. Butterflies flutter in my abdomen, and the warmth of his hand on my skin makes my stomach tighten. We emerge into a quiet corridor, and he nods down the hall. "This way."

I follow him blindly, trying my best to put one foot in front of the other while my mind races and my heart tries its best to explode out of my chest.

Everywhere his fingers touch, sparks dance across my skin. Heat curls in the pit of my stomach as he guides me down another hallway. I shouldn't be alone with him, because I know what's going to happen.

It's inevitable.

When the Prince pushes open a door, my pulse is hammering so hard I think I might pass out. He sweeps his arm around the room and grins at me.

"Welcome to my sanctuary."

We're in a medium-sized room. One wall is dominated with bookshelves, and there's a large, solid wood desk in the corner. Another corner has a couple of couches in it, with reading lamps arching over them. The middle of the room has a long table stretching across it, with chairs lining either side. It's lush and cozy.

"My study," the Prince says. "No one comes here."

The far wall is dominated by windows. I step lightly over to them, glancing out. The pristine, manicured royal gardens are splayed out below us.

"It's nice," I say. "Is this where your classes happen?"

"Most of them did," the Prince nods. "Although I've started my residency, so I'm working at the Farcliff General Hospital now."

"Imagine being sick and having royalty show up at your bedside," I laugh, glancing over my shoulder at him. "That's enough to give anyone a heart attack—if they haven't already had one." I walk over to the bookcases and run my fingers along the leather spines. "You'll make a special kind of doctor, that's for sure."

Prince Damon walks up behind me as I stare at the bookshelves and slides his hands over my hips. His chest presses up against my back, and heat ignites between my thighs.

I knew this would happen if I was alone with him. I knew I wouldn't be able to resist.

But I still followed him here.

I turn around in his arms to face him and slide my hands up his chest. He's warm, strong, and everything I've been missing. He smells exactly how I remember. My breath hitches, and I feel myself melting into his arms.

He's the sun, and I'm a fleck of space dust, caught in orbit around him. Of course I followed him here. Of course I couldn't resist him.

"It's good to see you," the Prince says in a low voice. "I've thought of that night a lot over the past few months."

"So have I."

"Why did you block my number?"

His fingers sink into my hips and my heart does a flip. "I was scared."

"Of my father?"

"Of my feelings," I whisper, dragging my eyes up to his. "We're not supposed to be together."

"Maybe before," Damon says, sliding his hands around to my ass, "but things have changed."

I want to believe him. Every fiber of my being wants it to be true. He's right—things have changed. The King has abdicated, the King's advisor has been charged with regicide. The Kingdom is in turmoil.

For me, turmoil is good. Turmoil means my mother might be able to come back to the Kingdom. Through what the investigation uncovers, it means I might find out exactly what happened. My family might finally find some peace.

Turmoil means that maybe—just maybe—I can be with Damon.

I curl my hands around the back of his neck and take a deep breath.

"You look beautiful today." Damon presses his hand against the bare skin of my lower back, slipping his fingers beneath my dress.

A spark travels up my spine, causing my head to angle up toward him. It's like my body is asking him to kiss me.

*Begging* him to kiss me.

No matter what's going on in my heart, no matter what

my mind is trying to make me do, I can't control what my body wants.

Damon knows it, and he crushes my lips with his own. He kisses me fiercely, sinking his fingers into my skin as a moan slips through my lips.

I want this. I want it so bad I'm trembling. The moment I walked into the Great Hall—into that room where Damon changed me all those months ago—I knew that I'd be in his arms before the night was over.

I'm sick of resisting, sick of trying to convince myself that I shouldn't do this, sick of torturing myself with thoughts of the Prince.

Damon is here. I'm here. We both want this.

I pull him closer, tangling my fingers into the hair at the nape of his neck. I roll my hips toward him. My back slams against the bookcase behind me. I wince.

"You okay?" Damon's eyebrows draw together.

"I'm good," I pant. My lips fly back to his. What is pain? Pain is nothing.

Pleasure is everything.

Before I know what I'm doing, my fingers are working to loosen his tie. I slide it off his neck and toss it aside. Damon's eyebrow arches and a grin curls his lips.

With trembling hands, I unbutton his shirt and push it off his shoulders. My eyes widen as I see mottled bruises covering his ribs, but Damon doesn't even seem to notice. He helps me tear the shirt off, flinging it behind him and kissing me again. His lips are on mine, and then on my jaw, my neck, my shoulder. He kisses my earlobe, scraping his teeth against it as he grinds himself against me.

All the while, I feel him pulsing against me, thick and hard. Oh, I feel him—and everything falls away.

I run my hands over every inch of him.

I've missed this.

I'm a sexual person, and I haven't slept with anyone in months. I haven't wanted to, but the need has still been there.

Right now, that need is cresting. My whole body is trembling, screaming for him to fuck me. My lips are swollen and wet with his kiss.

Damon spins me around without warning. I yelp, gripping onto the bookcase as his hand runs down my spine. He slides the straps of my dress off my shoulders, laying a soft kiss where the fabric used to be. I let it fall to my waist, arching my back and grinding my ass against him.

His cock is hard. He pushes it against me and my breath catches in my throat.

How many times have I thought of him like this? How many times have I given myself a less-than-satisfying orgasm while dreaming of this very situation?

Prince Damon's hands, broad and strong, slide down my sides and send shivers of pleasure running through my body. He presses his chest to my back, and the contact of his skin against mine makes my head spin. The Prince's hands run up my stomach to cup my breasts as he growls in my ear.

There are no words, but I know what that growl means. It means he feels exactly like I do. It means he, too, has dreamed of this.

With one hand still on my breast, he slips the other beneath my dress as it hangs from my waist. When his hand reaches my mound, it stops.

"No panties?" He rasps in my ear.

"Didn't want panty lines," I say, breathless. "It would ruin the look." My eyes are closed and all I can think about is his hand between my legs. It moves down a bit further, and his fingers tease my slit. I'm already soaking wet. I'm glad I have my back to him, because I'm blushing so hard my face probably matches my hair.

"No hair, either." His voice is breathy and heavy with need. "I won't be fucking a rainbow pussy this time." His finger slides between my legs and finds my bud.

My head is a mess.

"I got a wax yesterday," I say as my fingers dig into the bookcase. My cheeks are burning. "I don't know why... Is that okay?"

Damon lets out a deep, low chuckle. "Yes, it's okay—and I think I know why you did it, Dahlia."

"Why do you think?"

His fingers slide over and back through my slit as I continue to tremble against him. His other hand teases my breast as his lips brush over my neck. My wetness is almost embarrassing. I can feel it dripping down onto my legs as his hand slides further back toward my opening.

"You waxed that sweet, little pussy of yours because you knew you'd be getting fucked tonight." His voice is a low growl. It's commanding, and possessive, and rough—and it makes me whimper.

His finger slides into my opening, and my legs quake. He drags it in and out of me as his breath warms my neck and his cock pulses against my ass.

It's too much. It's not enough. I grip the shelves and gasp.

"You knew this would happen, or at least you hoped it would," he growls, his finger still stroking in and out of me.

The friction of his palm against my bud leaves me breathless, and I can't answer.

"You did it for me, didn't you?"

My fingers dig into the bookcase and I hold on as hard as I can. I don't trust my legs. Damon's cock presses against my ass as his fingers pump in and out of me. He pinches my nipple and I moan.

"Answer me, Princess. You hoped this would happen today."

"I told you," I pant. "I'm not a princess."

"You're my Princess." Damon drags his fingers out of me and moves them—soaked with my need—over my clit. I gasp, but I still can't answer. My forehead is resting against a book, and it's all I can do to stay standing.

"Say it, Dahlia," Damon growls. "Say you did this for me."

His hand moves faster, twirling over my bud as my wetness drips down my thighs. I squeeze my eyes shut and suck in a breath, and finally I can speak.

"Yes," I gasp. "I wanted you. I wanted this. I haven't stopped thinking about you since that night on the throne."

Damon spins me around and kisses me hard. His hands fumble to push my dress over the curve of my hips, and it puddles at my feet. I kick it away, clawing at him to bring him closer. The Prince crushes his lips against mine with a moan, kicking my legs apart and slipping his hand once more between them.

This is better than the first time. It's the culmination of months of waiting, wishing, hoping, anticipating. Prince Damon is stronger than I remembered. He's bigger. Rougher. More commanding.

I love every second of it.

When the Prince picks me up and wraps my legs around his waist, my heart does a flip. He claims my lips again, carrying me to the wide wooden desk. There, he sits me down on the edge and runs his hands over my body once again.

His body is chiseled to perfection. I want to ask him

where he got the cuts and bruises on his ribs and abdomen, but I don't have the chance.

"I've thought of this every single day for the past seven months," Prince Damon growls.

"I know," I breathe.

I watch him unfasten his belt and let his pants fall to the ground. When he drops his briefs down, too, his cock throbs toward me.

"I think he's saying hello," I laugh.

"He missed you," the Prince grins as he grasps his cock in his hand. His eyes darken as he moves closer to me. He brushes the tip of his cock against me, and I let out a long breath. I spread my legs wider as my breath hitches, the anticipation almost too much to handle.

"I don't have a condom," I say in a breathy voice as I sweep my eyes over his perfect body. "I'm not on the pill anymore."

"I'll pull out," the Prince answers.

It's not perfect, it's not foolproof, and I don't give a damn. His gorgeous cock is throbbing against me and I need it inside me. *Now.*

Prince Damon slides himself inside me inch by inch, stretching me wide as we both let out a low moan. It feels perfect. It feels like we were made for each other, like everyone who came before pales in comparison to him. He fits inside me so perfectly it makes me feel whole. Complete.

*Filled.*

We don't say a word from then on. His hands grip my thighs, my sides, my waist. I claw at his chest and pull his head down to kiss me. He thrusts inside me, deep and powerful and perfect. I moan into his shoulder, biting his skin and gasping as the pleasure mounts inside me.

It's more than pleasure. It's ecstasy. It's euphoria. It's every cell in my body aligning itself and screaming in unison as the Prince drives himself deeper and deeper inside me.

With rough, possessive hands, he pulls my hips closer to the edge of the desk. I lean back on my elbows and let my head fall back. His thumb finds my clit and I know I'm done.

My orgasm winds me. It rips the air out of my lungs and steals the scream from my lips. It stiffens every limb in my body and makes my walls contract around the Prince's shaft so tightly that I hear him groan in response.

Wildfire rips through my body from my center outward, spreading over every inch of me. The Prince thrusts himself inside me again and again as I try my best to ride my orgasm to the end.

I open my eyes and lift my head. My lips are open and I let out a moan as another wave of pleasure crashes into me. The Prince stares at me—at my chest, and my stomach, and down between my legs—and he grunts in response. His hands grip my legs and spread them wider, and I feel his cock start to throb.

He pulls his cock out of me and sprays his seed. White, sticky ropes cover my stomach, my breasts, all the way up to my chin. I watch him, body trembling...

...and I love it.

I love the messiness of it. I love him marking me like this—making me his. I like the feeling of his orgasm dripping off my body as my own pleasure subsides. His lips curl into a smile as he pumps the last of his cum onto my body, and then he drags his thumb through the mess, satisfied.

I'll never be anyone else's. I belong to Prince Damon, now and forever.

## 19

——

# DAMON

DAHLIA SMILES at me as she slips her dress back on. I hop on one foot as I pull my pants up, grinning back at her like a fool. I can't keep the smile off my face.

I've been dreaming of that for months now. Dreaming of *her*.

As much as I thought today would be difficult, and I didn't really want to celebrate when our whole family is in turmoil, it feels so fucking good to be with Dahlia that I don't care.

We toss out the tissues that we used to clean ourselves up with, and I wrap my arms around Dahlia's waist again. Laying a soft kiss on her lips, I sigh. It feels incredible to have her in my arms. I didn't know if I'd ever feel this again.

We make our way back to the wedding reception, where cocktails are already being served. Charlie sees us walk in, and his eyebrows shoot up a fraction of an inch.

Dahlia squeezes my arm. "I'd better go see Elle," she says, her cheeks flushing pink again. "I'll talk to you in a bit."

"Don't leave without saying goodbye."

"I'm not going anywhere." Her eyes sparkle. She smiles at me, and then ducks away.

I make my way over to Charlie, who's talking to his butler Neville. When I decided to go to medical school, I gave up my own personal butler. I figured if I'm giving up my royal life and living like a regular person, I needed to forego some of the royal privilege—including having staff. I don't mind, though. When I needed to sneak out of the castle without being noticed, not having a gaggle of employees following me around everywhere makes it a lot easier.

Charlie is glancing at a piece of paper that Neville handed him.

"We haven't been able to confirm that, sir," Neville says. He turns to me and gives me a low bow. "Prince Damon."

"Hey, Neville. What's this about?"

Charlie lets out a heavy sigh. "We're working through the evidence that we found on Mom's murder. So far, we can definitely confirm that Father and his advisor were involved. Aunt Mal, though, is another story. She wasn't in the country when Mom was murdered."

"Malerie hated Mom." I still remember the way my aunt looked at Dahlia, too, and I don't trust her.

"We were kids. We don't know that. And plus, even if she didn't like her, it doesn't mean she killed her." Charlie shakes his head, sighing. "Listen, Nev, I can't deal with this now. It's my wedding day."

"Sir, we've noticed that Lady Malerie seems to be making preparations to leave. If we don't act tonight, we may not have another chance to question her."

"I've already accused my father of murder, Nev. I don't want to arrest her without solid proof. I've only been King for two weeks, and I don't want to start my rule by making unlawful arrests."

"We can detain her without arresting her." Neville frowns. Even such a slight facial expression for him is a big deal. I can tell he wants Charlie to keep her in the country. "I don't trust her, Your Majesty."

Charlie lets out a heavy sigh. "She was there for us when Mom died, in her own way. She took care of Damon when he was bedridden after it happened. If I accuse her of being involved in this mess and it turns out she has nothing to do with it, she'll never forgive me."

"Sir..."

"I need to get back to my wedding." Charlie interrupts. Neville bows to us both and disappears. Unease snakes into my heart as I watch him walk away.

I'm inclined to agree with Charlie's butler. After the night in the throne room, my feelings about my aunt were tainted. Whereas before I thought of her as simply a slightly grumpy, slightly stuck-up old woman, after that evening, I'm not so sure. What do we really know about her, anyway?

If what Neville says is true, she's planning on leaving the Kingdom on Charlie's wedding night.

"Why isn't she here?" I ask. "I mean, if you still trust her, and you're not arresting her, why isn't she at your wedding?"

Charlie's face sours. "She refused the invitation. Look, I don't want to talk about this right now. I just want to enjoy my wedding, enjoy my bride, eat good food, and be happy for once. Is that too much to ask?"

He stares at me with hard eyes until I nod.

"You're right," I say. "I'm sorry."

Charlie takes a step toward Elle, who's talking excitedly with Dahlia. My brother pauses, glancing over his shoulder at me. His lips tug up at the corners.

"What's going on between you and Dahlia, anyway?"

"Nothing." I clear my throat, averting my eyes.

"Where did you disappear just now?"

"I was showing her my study. She said she was looking for somewhere to work that was off-campus."

"And you offered up your private study?"

"Yeah." I shrug, but I know Charlie doesn't believe me. That study is my sanctuary. I don't even let the maids touch it. No one goes in there except for me...

...and now Dahlia, too.

Charlie walks straight to Elle, near the head table, and turns to our small gathering of guests. He raises his arms and clears his throat. As King, that's enough to make the entire room fall silent.

He's definitely got the aura of a king about him. He's slid into his role with ease, and I'm happy for him. Charlie hooks his arm around his bride, and she gazes up at him with a soft smile on her lips.

They've found their way to each other, and even amidst the strife in our family, they look happy.

Maybe happiness is possible for Gabe and me, too. Maybe we can all get past this. My eyes move to Dahlia, and my heart jumps in my chest.

Charlie turns to the guests. "Thank you for coming tonight," he starts. All of us shift and turn toward him, and he continues with a smile on his face. "It means the world to Elle and me that you'd be here to watch us join our lives and families together. We couldn't think of a better way of celebrating our marriage than with the few people in this room."

Applause fills the room, and Charlie raises his arms to accept it. Watching him makes me proud to be his brother— proud that he's our King. A lump forms in my throat as emotion starts to choke me. Farcliff is entering a new era, and I can't help but feel hopeful.

Charlie's eyes swing to Dahlia. His smile widens. "Miss Raventhal, you've been supportive of Elle for many years. The

Kingdom hasn't been kind to you or your family, and I would like to officially extend my sincere apologies, and my hope for reconciliation."

Silence settles over the room. Dahlia nods her head, her eyes widening. I can tell she's uncomfortable.

Charlie takes a deep breath. "The official correspondence is already in the mail, but I wanted to tell you here, first: I've invited your parents back to Farcliff, and I hope it will be the new beginning that we all need to move beyond the past, and create a happier, more open future for all of the Kingdom."

He finishes his speech strong, and the room erupts in applause. I clap along with the rest of them, but my eyes are on Dahlia. She looks more worried than happy, and I wish I was beside her to comfort her.

I know what she's been through—how she grew up, and how deep her fear of Farcliff runs—and I know this can't be easy. If Charlie wants to start a reconciliation with the Raventhals, he doesn't know how much of an uphill battle he has ahead of him.

But King Charlie is oblivious. He laps up the applause and wraps his arms around a stunned Dahlia. Then, he turns to Elle and motions for us all to take our seats for dinner.

I'm sitting at the opposite end of the table to Dahlia, but I still steal a couple of glances her way. Her eyebrows are drawn together, and her hand trembles whenever she brings her glass of wine to her lips.

My heart squeezes, and the dread in my stomach grows stronger. Charlie may think the past is behind us, but I know it won't be that easy to leave it in our wake.

# 20

## LADY MALERIE

STANDING IN A DOORWAY, Malerie hears the new King's speech, and her heart sinks. Inviting the Raventhals back into Farcliff is like a death sentence.

The Queen would still be alive if it weren't for Tabitha Raventhal. Malerie doesn't believe the accusations against the former King. He might be brutish and violent, but her brother is not a killer.

No—this was the Raventhals.

Now, the former King is under house arrest—well, castle arrest—and the Kingdom is upside down. To add insult to injury, the fucking Raventhals are back?

Malerie glances at Damon, who's busy staring at Dahlia. Anger flares in her heart, and she turns away from the wedding, walking away from whatever remains of her family.

# 21

# DAHLIA

I'VE NEVER BEEN to a royal wedding before, and after my first dinner party at the castle, I was looking forward to the food tonight. As it stands, though, I don't taste a single bite.

All I can think of is my mother and father, and how much they'll freak out when they get their official invitation back to Farcliff. It won't be as easy as King Charlie thinks to get my parents—especially my mother—to come back to the Kingdom. Not by a long shot.

But Elle and the new King are besotted with each other, and I won't be one to make a scene. So, instead, I just sit beside Elle and push my food around my plate. I twirl my finger into the pink tips of my hair and try to look less miserable than I feel.

In my mind, I know these are all good things. I know the investigation into the death of the Queen will bring about change in Farcliff. I know that Charlie will be a good King.

It's just that my family has been through so much. I've spent my whole life in fear of the royal family, and now I'm just supposed to forget about it all?

I'm supposed to run into Damon's arms, and trust Charlie to do the right thing?

Power corrupts people, and the Crown weighs heavy. How do I know that these people will do right by my family? How do we really know that what the investigation uncovers won't be swept up under the rug, and my family will be the scapegoats once again?

Elle touches my arm. "You okay? I thought you'd be happy about this."

I force a smile. "Of course I'm happy, Elle. This will change everything."

Someone else calls for Elle's attention, and I turn my gaze back to my full plate of food. One of the waiters appears by my side and takes away my uneaten plate, dropping off another course that I already know I won't touch.

I push my chair back. Elle glances at me, frowning.

"Bathroom," I explain.

She nods.

I slip out of the reception room through the first door I find. It's hard to get a full breath, and my head feels like it's full of cotton balls. I yelp when I feel a hand on my back.

"Sorry!" Damon says, pulling his hand away. "Didn't mean to startle you."

"I didn't hear you behind me."

"I just wanted to make sure you're okay." His eyebrows draw together and he stares into my eyes.

I take a deep breath and lean against the hallway wall, putting a hand to my forehead. "Yeah, I'm okay. I just got a bit overwhelmed in there. It's like I'm supposed to just pretend that everything is okay now that the King is gone. I mean... I'm sorry. I didn't mean that in a bad way, I just..."

"I know," Damon says. "Things that have hurt you before don't just go away because someone pretends to wave a magic wand. Believe me, I know how that feels. This whole wedding is a bit surreal."

"Exactly! I grew up my entire life scared of this place…" I inhale sharply and shake my head. "It's hard to get over that."

"Well, maybe *don't* try to get over it." Damon leans on the wall beside me. "Maybe you should just accept it for now."

"What do you mean?"

"Some things hurt. They cut you deep, and it's not easy to let go of them." His voice trails off and he stares into nothing, retreating into his own thoughts.

I think about the bruises on his body, and I wonder what exactly he's thinking about. I've spent enough time with the Prince to know that there's more to him than meets the eye, but who he is deep down to the core is still a mystery to me. He's good, I think. I can see that in him, but his scars aren't only physical.

The Prince inhales and glances at me. "You ready to go back in there?"

"Do I have to?"

He chuckles. "Unfortunately, yes. Oh, and I told Charlie that you were wanting a study space, so I offered up my library. You know, in case he asks."

"Thanks for the heads up," I grin. "What if I wanted to come back and study some more?"

"Dahlia, you can study with me anytime." He growls, sweeping his hand into my hair and kissing me. A noise at the far end of the hall cuts our kiss short, and we head back into the main room.

I don't even know why we're hiding anymore—there's no reason for us to pretend we're not into each other. Damon and I seem to be on the same page, though, and I'm glad he wants to take things slow.

For the rest of the evening, Prince Damon doesn't stray

too far away from me. It's as if there's an invisible string holding us close to each other. I can feel his movements before I see them. I can sense his gaze whenever it lands on me.

I like the feeling. No—I *love* it. I love knowing that he's near, that he's looking at me. I love when his fingers slide over the small of my back.

When the dancing starts, Damon is right there in front of me with his hand extended. He pulls me close to his chest and holds me there in the middle of the dance floor. We stay stuck to each other for three, four, five songs, until I finally pull away.

My eyes are shining, and I can't keep the smile off my face. We haven't said much to each other, but I feel like we understand each other on a deep, unspoken level.

I sit down at my chair and nibble on some wedding cake. Elle sits down beside me, her cheeks flushed and her eyes bright. "So, you and Damon, huh?"

I shake my head. "Don't know what you're talking about."

"Is this why you've been so quiet the past few months? How long has this been going on?"

"Nothing is going on, Elle." I steal a glance toward Damon, who's talking to another guest.

"Uh huh," Elle says. I glance over to see her rolling her eyes. "Now I understand how frustrating it must have been to see me with Charlie a few months ago," she laughs. "You just won't admit to yourself that you like Prince Damon."

"He's okay," I grin.

"Have you..."

"Have I what?"

She wiggles her eyebrows. "You know."

"God, no! Elle!" My face turns bright read and I bury my face in my wine.

Elle laughs, leaning back in her chair and sweeping her hands over her pregnant stomach. She shakes her head. "You're a terrible liar, Dahlia. Plus, the first two years we lived together, you broke three bed frames. I haven't been woken up by squeaking bed springs in months!"

"I'm exploring celibacy."

Elle's eyes flash. "You like him, don't you?"

"Of course not."

"You like him *a lot*."

"Why are we talking about this?" I laugh, shaking my head. "Nothing is going on! We should be talking about you and Charlie. We should be celebrating your wedding and your new baby."

"I like to celebrate love in all its forms, Dahlia, including young love and new, budding relationships."

"Shut up," I say, shaking my head. "It's nothing. Prince Damon is cute, that's all."

Elle purses her lips and shakes her head. "Well, well, well, the tables have turned. Now, I'm not the one blushing anymore."

I laugh, putting my hands to my cheeks to hide the redness. My thoughts flick back to the study, and then to the throne, and to the thousands of dirty thoughts I've had in between.

"You're screwed," Elle says with a laugh. "You like him. You're in so much trouble."

I glance at her and take a deep breath. I let it out without answering, but I know she's right. I like him a lot, which means I'm completely, royally screwed.

# 22

# DAMON

THIS TIME, I'm not going to let Dahlia get away from me. The Raventhals are officially welcome in Farcliff now, which means she has no excuse. She can't run away from me again.

The day after the wedding, I show up on her front doorstep. No more waiting and hoping for her to call. No more putting the ball in her court.

I want her, and I will have her.

Dahlia opens the door and her eyes widen. "Your Highness! What are you doing here?"

"Call me Damon, Dahlia. I would hope we're past formalities by now."

"Fine. Damon, what are you doing here?" She grins, opening the door wider. I step inside. She motions toward the kitchen and I follow her. She's wearing that sparkly purple robe again, and I remember the very first time I saw her, and how much I wanted to tear that robe off her body.

Maybe today will be the day.

"Coffee?" She motions to the machine.

"Please."

I watch her put the coffee on, and then she leans against

the kitchen counter and stares at me. "What can I do for you?"

"I was hoping you'd stay at the castle last night. You disappeared before I could talk to you again. I asked you not to leave without saying goodbye."

"That was by design," she laughs. "You're too persuasive for your own good."

I take a deep breath. I've been rehearsing a speech in my head all morning, and now it's time to deliver it. The thought of letting Dahlia slip through my fingers again is unbearable, and I can't let it happen.

"Dahlia, look. I know you have reservations about going to the Farcliff Castle, and I understand that. I know you don't trust me or my family, and I'm not trying to pressure you into anything. I was hoping—"

"What are the bruises on your body from?"

I pause. Neither of us say anything. The coffee machine gurgles.

"Nothing." My back stiffens and I force myself to hold her gaze.

"So, you're telling me that I should trust you, but you won't tell me why every time I see your bare chest, it looks like you've been beaten to a pulp the week before?"

My ears burn. I try to swallow past a lump in my throat as my mind races. This wasn't part of the script I'd planned out in my head. This wasn't part of the plan.

Dahlia arches an eyebrow.

In that moment, I know I have two choices. I can lie and protect myself—and potentially lose any chance I have with Dahlia...

...or I can tell the truth.

"I pay a man in Grimdale to beat me."

My voice is flat and emotionless. I hold Dahlia's gaze

without wavering as the weight of my words settles between us.

I've never told anyone that before. I've never even considered telling someone. It's my biggest secret, my biggest shame.

Yet, telling Dahlia was easy.

Her brows draw together and a couple of lines appear in her forehead. The coffee is ready, but both of us ignore it. Dahlia grips her bathrobe tighter around her chest and stares at me.

"What do you mean?" She asks softly.

"I mean that whenever things get too much, when I find myself in a deep, dark hole, I go to a warehouse in Grimdale and I pay someone to beat the shit out of me. He doesn't touch my face. No one knows."

I should be embarrassed, but I'm not. I sit a little taller, watching her. Dahlia pads lightly toward me and puts her hands on either side of my face. She tilts her head up toward me, staring deep into my eyes.

"Why in the world would you do that?" Her voice is husky, barely above a whisper.

My heart thumps. I shrug. "It's the only way to think clearly when it all gets too much. I don't know how to explain it."

"Oh, Damon," she says softly. Sadness fills her eyes and I shake my head.

"That's not why I told you. I didn't tell you so that you'd feel sorry for me. I've never told anyone this, Dahlia, but I told you because I want you to trust me. When you walked away from me before..." I suck a breath in through my teeth. "...it nearly killed me. I can't explain it. I know I'm coming on too strong. I don't want to freak you out. I just..."

As I search for the right words, Dahlia presses her lips to

mine. She sits down across my lap and pulls me closer, sighing against me.

All the confusion, the doubts, the fear—they all evaporate.

My heart soars.

I wrap her in my arms, holding her close to me as I claim her lips. She feels tiny in my lap—and so fucking perfect it shouldn't even be possible.

I've never told anyone about my beatings before, and I'd never intended to. I thought when I stopped needing them, I'd stop going to see Nigel, and that would be the end of it. I thought I'd never be comfortable enough with a woman to tell her. I thought I'd live with my broken, dark heart forever.

Telling Dahlia the truth stitched a part of my heart back together.

She pulls away from me, her hands still resting on my face. Dahlia gazes deep into my eyes.

"I want you to stop doing that to yourself."

"Okay."

"I mean, it, Damon. This thing between us…" She takes a deep breath. "It shouldn't feel so right, but it does. I want to keep seeing you, but I want you to stop hurting yourself."

In this moment, I'd promise her anything. I'd say anything to taste her lips again—but the way she's looking at me makes me pause.

For the first time in many, many years, I consider what she's saying. What would happen if I were to stop? What would happen if I never went to Nigel again? What would happen if I had to deal with the Darkness on my own?

"Whatever it is inside you that makes you do that, I'll help you with it," Dahlia says softly, answering my unsaid questions. It's like she can feel the buzzing in my head, and she knows exactly what to say to make it quiet down.

I gulp, and finally nod my head. "Okay."

"You'll stop?"

"Yeah."

"Good." Dahlia rests her head on my shoulder and takes a deep breath. She melts into my arms, and we sit there for a few moments without saying anything.

It feels so good to have her here like this. This is where she's supposed to be—where *I'm* supposed to be. I close my eyes and squeeze my arms around her, trying to understand these feelings inside me.

Whatever this is between us—this chemistry, this spark—it's *real*. We can both feel it, and we both want to pursue it. Even after months apart, it feels like no time has passed at all.

That has to mean something, right? That has to be worth fighting for? Worth being honest for? Worth changing for?

I tilt her chin up toward me and I kiss her gently, feeling her body quiver against mine. As I kiss her there in the kitchen where I first met her, I know that there's no turning back. Even if I wanted to leave, something has changed between us.

There's no more running, no more secrets, no more tangled family pasts to keep us apart. For the first time, Dahlia and I can be open with each other. We can face our deepest fears—together. Me with my own demons, and Dahlia with her family's past.

Everything clicks into place, and it's not about crazy sex and burning passion—it's about us, together. Nothing more, and nothing less.

# 23

# DAHLIA

AUNT THERESA IS RIGHT. I can't live my life in fear of some stupid, non-existent curse, or keep worrying about what my family thinks. I need to make decisions for myself—and not just my hair color. I need to decide how I want to live my life, and who I want to live it with.

Not to mention Prince Damon is very convincing. His kiss is, at least—and his touch. I rest my head against his shoulder and let out a sigh.

"So, we're doing this?" I ask in a small voice.

"We're doing this."

"You're not worried about dating a Raventhal?"

"Not in the slightest." Damon chuckles, smoothing his hand over my hair. He kisses my forehead and I sigh into his chest. It feels good to be in his arms. It's warm, safe, and comforting. It's home.

I take a deep breath. I feel like I need to say it out loud to prove to myself that I can.

"What if I told you I'm cursed? That everything in my life ends up going wrong, and that it's always been this way?"

"Maybe we're both cursed, and our curses will cancel

each other out," Damon says. I can hear the grin in his voice. He kisses my forehead again and I lean back to stare into his eyes.

"This curse is no joke." I say, keeping my face serious. "You could be getting yourself in a whole heap of trouble."

"Maybe I like trouble." The Prince's eyes flash. He pauses, tilting his head. "Wait, are you being serious right now?"

I bite my lip, blushing. "I know it sounds crazy."

"Is this why you didn't want to see me before? Do you really think you're cursed?"

I shake my head. "I don't know what I think anymore. My mother used to say it to me when I was younger. It just stayed with me, I guess."

"That's a bit..." He frowns.

"A bit what?"

"Well, manipulative."

I frown, considering his words. "I don't know if I'd go so far as to call it manipulative."

"Telling a small child that she's cursed, to the point where she carries that shit into adulthood? That's kind of fucked up, don't you think? I don't know. I'm no expert in healthy parent-child relationships, but that seems weird to me."

I chew my lip, nodding. "Yeah."

My instinct is to defend my mother—it's what I always do. But when I stop and think about Damon's words, it makes me realize that he might have a point. This curse has always hung over my head—just like my fear of Farcliff.

Damon chuckles and kisses the tip of my nose. "I'll risk a curse if it means I get to be with you." I yelp as he scoops me up and throws me over his shoulder. He carries me to my bedroom and kicks the door closed behind us.

Laughing, I wriggle in his arms until he drops me on the

bed. His eyes are heady and his lips are too tempting to resist. I wrap my arms around him and melt into his embrace.

This time, we use protection, and I vow to go and pick up a new birth control prescription as soon as possible. Having unprotected sex in his study was irresponsible. I know it was, but I just can't bring myself to regret it.


THE PRINCE SURPRISES me when he agrees to sleep over at my dumpy Grimdale house. I'm lying on his chest, drawing circles with my fingertips over his skin.

"Are you sure this is luxurious enough for you?" I ask, grinning.

"Being with you is luxurious, Dahlia. I don't need a feather bed."

I smile, inhaling the scent of his skin. "You could be the Prince and the Pea for all I know. Maybe you won't be able to sleep a wink in this shack of mine. You'll feel every spring in my old mattress."

"I don't intend on sleeping, but it won't be because the mattress isn't soft enough," the Prince growls, flipping me onto my back.

I squeal and giggle, wrapping my arms around him. He props himself up on his elbows and strokes my hair, sighing.

"I'm happy when I'm with you, Dahlia."

I stroke the side of his face. "*One should never direct people towards happiness, because happiness too is an idol of the marketplace. One should direct them towards mutual affection.*" I stretch my head up to kiss his neck. "*A beast gnawing at its prey can be happy too, but only human beings can feel affection for each other, and this is the highest achievement they can aspire to.*"

Damon struggles to fight the smile off his face. "And which Russian novelist said that?"

"Aleksandr Solzhenitsyn."

"Well," Damon says, sliding off to my side and lifting me up to straddle him. "Then, I feel affection for you, Dahlia, and I hope that the feeling is mutual. Does Alexander Whatshisname approve of that?"

"He's dead, so I can't ask him," I grin, "but I'm sure he would."

"How do you remember these quotes off the top of your head? Maybe you should be studying literature."

I shrug. "Our brains just remember things we're interested in."

The Prince's eyes soften, and his fingers sink into my thighs. My heart thumps.

Turns out, the Prince is right. Neither of us sleep a wink that night.

I should know that something bad will happen. I should be prepared for it.

I've said it before—I'm cursed, even if I don't quite believe it anymore.

But do I think of the curse when Damon sweeps me off my feet and makes me feel like the most beautiful girl in the world?

No, of course not.

I should know that anytime something good happens, something bad is sure to follow.

And things with Damon are very, very good. I can't keep the smile off my face. I rush home after class and find him in my house, and then we fall into bed together. I wake up tangled in his arms, and my heart soars.

I forget about my past, about my family name, about the curse. I forget about my mother, and about the Queen.

I forget about everything except the Prince—the way he looks, the way he moves, the way he makes me feel.

It's euphoric. It's magic. He knows all my buttons, and pushes them gladly, as if we've lived a thousand lifetimes together.

In reality, it's only been a couple of weeks. But Damon starts sleeping over at my place, and we fall into an easy routine. I've never had anything happen so easily. Once I let go of my fears, it just feels right.

My studies are going well, and my internship at the university lab is fascinating. I haven't dropped anything, or slipped on any banana peels, or had any bad luck in weeks.

Even with precise lab work, I can pipette and decant and do everything with a steady hand. My first week at the lab, I smashed four glass beakers. Since I've been with Damon, I haven't broken a single one.

He's equally as busy with his residency, and I admire him for it. I know it's not easy for him to give up his royal life in order to serve as a doctor—and he gets a lot of pushback for it both inside and outside the castle walls. To his credit, he keeps going.

Usually, Damon sleeps over at my place. He bought me some better pillows and fixed the leaky faucet in the bathroom.

It's... *nice*. It's natural. It's easy. My heart beats for him, and I live two weeks in complete bliss.


BUT ALL GOOD things must come to an end. In my case, it's not so much an *end* as a snap back to my eternally cursed reality.

Two weeks after Prince Damon moves in with me, I finally make it to the doctor to refill my birth control prescription.

Doctor Nokes leads me into her examination room and motions to a chair. She has bright blue-rimmed glasses perched on the end of her nose, and she always wears a kind smile. She's never judged me or made me feel uncomfortable, which is why I've kept coming back to her. Today, though, my heart is beating a little faster than usual and I'm not sure why.

The doctor taps on her computer to pull up my file. "Okay, Dahlia, looks like it's time for a pelvic exam. I'll have to do one before I can give you a new prescription. We can do it right now, if you like."

I smile. "Sure."

Dr. Nokes gives me a couple of minutes to strip down and get ready. The examination table has white paper laid over it, and it crunches as I sit down. I lay the sheet she left for me over my lap and stare at the ceiling, waiting. A soft knock on the door sounds, and the doctor comes back in.

"Ready?"

"As ready as ever." I force a smile, but my nerves are cranking tighter.

Dr. Nokes swings the stirrups over and directs me to scoot down to the edge of the table. I've done this dozens of times for Pap smears, and I shouldn't be nervous—but when Dr. Nokes inserts the speculum, fear clenches in my stomach.

The doctor makes a soft noise, and my heart starts to thump. She pokes her eyes up above my knees and tilts her head.

"Dahlia, is there any chance that you're pregnant?"

# 24

# DAMON

MEDICAL RESIDENCY IS TOUGH. Add on top of that an inquest into my mother's death, the disgrace of my father, a new monarch for the Kingdom of Farcliff, *and* a new girlfriend for me. I've got a lot on my plate right now.

Maybe that's why I don't notice a change in Dahlia right away.

After two weeks together full of studying, sex, and very little sleep, I'm put on the night shift. I come back to her place —it's starting to feel more like our place—and slump down on her sofa.

"I'm on a two-week night rotation at the hospital starting tomorrow," I tell her. "After that, I'm back to days."

"Night shift," she says, sticking out her tongue. "That sucks."

"We might not get to see very much of each other."

"I feel like I'm on night shift already." Dahlia laughs. "Haven't had a full night's sleep since you started staying here."

Her face looks lined, and she glances away from me. Am I imagining things, or has something shifted between us?

Maybe she doesn't want me to move in as quickly as I have. Maybe she wants some space. My chest tightens at the thought—irrationally, I know. Everyone needs space. The last thing I want to do is crowd her.

We've been spending every spare moment together, and I haven't felt this good in years. Even a subtle shift in her demeanor is troubling to me. I open my mouth to ask her about it, but I don't get the chance.

Dahlia takes a deep breath and stands up, brushing lint off her shirt and heading toward the kitchen. "You okay with leftovers tonight?"

"Yeah," I answer, following her. "That's fine."

She opens the fridge without looking at me. There's tightness in her shoulders, and I watch her avoid my gaze.

"Dahlia, is everything okay?"

She pauses what she's doing and turns toward me. With a deep breath, she lifts her eyes up to me and opens her mouth.

Nothing comes out.

I wait for her to speak, and she finally sighs. "Yeah," she says. "Everything's fine."

Dahlia walks up to me and wraps her arms around my waist. She buries her face in my chest and lets out a long breath. I squeeze my arms around her.

"Are you sure?"

She nods, saying a muffled 'yes' into my chest. When she pulls away again, the tightness is gone from her face and she nods toward the food.

"Let's eat. I'm starving."

I eat, and Dahlia pushes food around her plate. I frown, but I can tell she doesn't want to talk to me about whatever is bothering her, so I don't push it.

We've only really been together for a couple of weeks. I

don't know all her moods yet, or how to react when something is bothering her.

So, I do what I like people to do for me. I give her some space.

We don't say much to each other that evening, and we go to bed early. She gives me a kiss before heading to her classes, and I hang around the house until it's time for my shift in the evening.

I'm gone before she comes back, and then I'm too busy at the hospital to think about what's happening between us. Emergency medicine takes a lot more mental and physical energy than I ever would have imagined. I'm running around all night, trying my best to do whatever my attending physician needs of me.

When the sun comes up, I'm doing mountains of paperwork.

By the time I get home, Dahlia is already gone off to her classes. I collapse into bed and fall asleep.

I don't see Dahlia for three days, because we're always missing each other.

ON THE FOURTH DAY, I come home a bit earlier and catch Dahlia getting ready for her day. I wrap my arms around her and inhale the scent of her hair.

"I've missed you," I groan.

"Me too," she says, kissing me gently. She nods to her phone. "Elle just called. She gave birth to baby Charlie."

My eyes widen. "Already?"

"Right on time," Dahlia smiles. "Today was her due date. I'm skipping my morning classes to go see her."

"Can you hold off for half an hour? I'll come, too. Just have to shower and call Charlie."

Dahlia nods. She has the same tightness around her eyes as she did early in the week, and her face is still shuttered. But she kisses me gently and wraps her arms around me, and my fears start to melt away. Maybe we're both just tired.

The darkness in my heart loves to needle at my insecurities, though, and I wonder if there's more to it than just fatigue. Maybe she's second-guessing this relationship? Maybe she's not happy with me after all?

I shake the thoughts away. I know what self-sabotage feels like.

We're probably both just exhausted.

ELLE GIVES birth at the Farcliff Royal Hospital. It's closer to the castle than Farcliff General, and is where all the monarchs have given birth in the past. Dahlia and I make our way to her room and are ushered in by a glowing midwife. "Congratulations, sir," she says. "You're an uncle."

Dahlia goes to Elle, and Charlie stands up from a chair. I shake his hand, smiling. "Congrats, Your Majesty."

"Thanks, Damon," he smiles. His baby is cooing in its bassinet by the bed, and Charlie strokes the baby's cheek. "Elle was fantastic."

"You? Not so much," our new Queen smiles. "Charlie passed out."

"That is officially a state secret," Charlie laughs. "That does not leave this room."

"You didn't!" Dahlia exclaims, laughing.

"There was more blood than I was expecting," Charlie says.

Dahlia goes to the new baby and lets out a soft sigh. Her hand drifts to her own stomach, and her eyes soften. Feeling my gaze, she lifts her eyes up to mine.

For the first time all week, a genuine smile stretches across her lips.

"You want to hold him?" Elle asks.

Dahlia sucks a breath in. "Can I? I'm scared."

"Don't be," Elle grins. "He's only the heir to the throne."

Dahlia giggles and reaches for the baby.

"Support his neck," Elle instructs. She's smiling, staring at her new son like only a mother can.

Dahlia has a similar look on her face. She looks so happy, holding that baby, and it makes my heart skip a beat. For a fraction of a second, it looks like Dahlia is holding her own child.

It makes my mind rush in a million different directions. Is that what I want?

A lump forms in my throat as I watch Dahlia with the baby. There's so much joy in this room, and Dahlia looks so natural as she holds the newborn. She rocks him and lays a kiss on the baby's forehead.

Glancing at me again, she gives me a shy smile.

I gulp.

A part of me wants that—a part of me would put a baby in Dahlia's womb right now. I'd be a father to our child. I'd love her until the ends of the earth.

But another, bigger part of me hesitates. I'm not ready to be a father. I barely even know Dahlia! Plus, there's so much damage inside me that I don't even know that I *could* be a parent.

I'm not fit to be a father. I've always known it. There's too much badness inside me, too much scar tissue. I couldn't. I can't. I won't.

My heart starts to thump, and suddenly I need some air.

I duck out of the room and lean against the wall, taking

long, slow breaths until my heartbeat quiets down. After a few minutes, Dahlia appears in front of me.

"Are you okay?"

"Yeah," I sigh. "My mind just started going crazy there. I started thinking about having kids and..." I shake my head.

"And...?"

"And, well, I'm glad we're not having any right now." I laugh, shaking my head.

Dahlia's face falls. "You don't want kids?"

"No! I do! It's just... I don't know." I put my hand to her waist and Dahlia pulls away ever so slightly. She looks devastated.

I clear my throat. "Not right now. It's not... How would we..."

"I get it," she says, nodding quickly. "Yeah." Dahlia glances up at me and then away again. "I'd better go back in there."

She slips away from me without saying another word. I've done something wrong, but I don't know what.

Just like that, in two or three minutes, I know that something has shifted between us. The happy, domestic life that we've been living for the past few weeks shimmers in my mind as if it were all a mirage.

25

———

## DAHLIA

He doesn't want kids. The father of my child doesn't want a baby.

I drift through the day, doing my best to act normal, even though everything inside me is crumbling.

Ever since I found out I was pregnant, I've felt like I'm walking a tightrope. At any second, I'm going to fall down, down, down. Hearing Damon say he doesn't want kids made me wobble, and I try my best to keep it together.

I'm pregnant. Even thinking the words makes my heart thump harder. It had to be the day in the study, at the royal wedding. I've been wracking my brain, trying to figure out how this happened. We've been safe every time except for that day.

I can't believe this is happening. When Elle got pregnant, I thought she was the most irresponsible person in Farcliff. I never thought it would happen to me.

How could I be so stupid?

Damon and I make our way back to the house in silence, and all the while I'm pretending that I'm not coming apart at the seams.

165

The Prince says a few words to me, and goes into the bedroom to sleep before his next shift. I mumble a response and watch him walk away, and my heart turns black in my chest.

I lounge on the couch and run my hand over my stomach.

I'm *pregnant*. Squeezing my eyes shut, I let out a sigh and slump down.

I thought everything was going well. I thought my life was starting to look up, and that Damon and I had a chance at happiness. I even thought that my family would be able to come back to Farcliff.

I thought I'd live happily ever after.

*Ha!*

Panic starts to well up inside me. My mind races a million miles an hour, thinking of every possibility in my future.

Getting rid of the baby—adoption or otherwise—is out of the question. Even a few weeks in, I know this baby is mine to keep. In a flash, I understand how Elle felt just a few months ago.

The Prince doesn't want kids. My parents would have a fit if they knew I was having a Prince of Farcliff's baby.

So, what choice am I left with? Lie to my parents? Lie to Damon, and do this on my own? Tell them, and risk the fall-out? Disappear back to the Rocky Mountains and pretend this never happened?

My heart squeezes, and I do my best to take a full breath.

I jump when knock comes on my door. Sitting on the couch, I stare down the hall without moving. I'm not answering the door. I don't care if it's the King of Farcliff himself, I'm not talking to anyone.

No way.

They knock again, a bit louder this time. I sigh as I heave

myself off the couch, trudging down the hallway. Whoever it is, I'll just tell them to leave.

But then, I open the door to see my mother and father standing on my creaky old stoop. My heart sinks. I'd forgotten they were invited to the Farcliff Castle, and now with baby Charlie being born, it's the perfect opportunity for this reconciliation to begin.

Wonderful.

I can't wait for us to be one big, happy fucking family again.

I say a silent prayer of thanks that Damon is sleeping, but my palms still start to sweat. I know that my parents are nervous about coming back to Farcliff—how would they react if they knew Damon and I were seeing each other?

How would they react if they knew he was sleeping in my bed?

How would they react if they knew I was *carrying his child*?

"Darling, is this where you live? You could have asked us for money," my mother says, her eyebrows drawing together. She looks at the front porch, rotting and falling apart in places and then sweeps her eyes over the front yard. I feel like crying.

I've never been embarrassed of my home, but there are too many emotions swirling inside me.

"Nice to see you too, Mom." I lean over to kiss her cheek. My father wraps me in a tight embrace before pulling back with his hands on my shoulders. He studies my face, frowning.

"Your mother is right, Dahlia. You can't live in a place like this."

"Like what?" My spine stiffens. How dare they come here and criticize my house like this? They shipped me off to the mountains to be homeschooled by my aunts, but now, all of a sudden, I'm too good for Grimdale? Now, all of a sudden, I'm a Raventhal again?

Anger spikes through me and it takes me a moment to catch my breath. I don't know why I'm feeling defensive about this house, but it's been my home for over two years. With Elle gone up to the castle, and my love life taking a sharp turn toward *disaster*, this house is the last familiar thing that I have.

"Maybe we should get a hotel, Harry." My mother glances around the neighborhood, and frustration bubbles up inside me. They didn't mind me living in a shack in the woods until I was sixteen, but apparently when I'm in Farcliff, I'm supposed to live in the lap of luxury.

"You guys want to come in?" I ask, pulling the door open wider. Defiance makes me jut my chin out. Let them find out about me and Damon. Maybe I'll tell them all about the baby! They probably wouldn't care about a few rotten planks of wood on my front stoop if they knew about that!

My father glances at me, and then he looks at my mother. "We tried, remember? Everywhere is booked up. People have come from all around for the birth of the Prince. The King invited us to stay at the palace, Tabitha," my father continues. "We should accept the invitation. They're expecting us today."

My mother wrings her hands in front of her, biting her lip.

I take a deep breath to compose myself. My emotions are cranked up to a hundred right now, and I need to remember who I'm talking to. My parents have been away from Farcliff for years. Of course they're worried about me, and about themselves.

"Tell you what," I say. "I'll come up to the castle with you.

All three of us can stay there. Elle said she'd appreciate some help with the baby, and it's closer to campus."

Not to mention, that means they won't be staying at my place—and they won't know about Damon just yet. They'll get to stay in nicer accommodation, and I'll have time to figure out how to break it to them that I'm falling in love with one of the Princes...

... Oh, and that I'm pregnant.

Holy Farcliff, how will I tell Damon? My stomach clenches, and I feel like I'm going to throw up. I can't keep up with this roller coaster. Is this what they mean when they talk about pregnancy hormones? Am I going to spend the next eight months struggling to keep up with my own emotions?

"I don't know," my mother says, shifting her weight from foot to foot.

I force a smile. "It's fine. I've met the royal family, and my best friend Elle is the Queen now. It's safe over there."

"My best friend was the Queen, too," Mom snaps. My father squeezes her hand and they exchange a loaded look. They've probably talked about this a million times.

My mother straightens her shoulders. "Okay. Fine."

"I have class in an hour, but I'll meet you there tonight, okay?"

My mother lets out a sigh and nods. "Okay. It's good to see you, Dahlia." She wraps me in another hug. She holds me tight, and it takes all my self-control to not break down in her arms.

What if I did tell them? What if I blurted it out—blurted everything out about Damon, and the baby, and how I feel about it all?

Maybe they would help me.

But my mother pulls away and takes a deep breath. She forces a smile and nods to me. "See you tonight."

I watch them walk away, and my lips stay sealed.

Damon wakes up around four o'clock looking tired as hell. I'm waiting for him in the kitchen when he stumbles out.

"I made you lunch for your shift."

"Thanks, babe," Damon says, kissing my forehead. "That's nice of you."

"Also… I'm moving up to the castle." *And I'm pregnant, and you're the father.* "My parents want me to go up with them. Moral support, I guess."

Damon frowns. He's still groggy, and I can tell he doesn't understand what's going on. "Okay—but I thought you hated the castle."

"I don't hate it. It's just… My parents are in town. They'll only go up there if I'm with them."

Damon rakes his fingers through his hair and takes a deep breath. "All right. Did you tell them about me?"

I bite my lip. "Not exactly."

"Not exactly as in 'no'?"

I snort. "Yeah."

"Are you embarrassed of me?"

"No! Not at all. It's just that it's hard enough for my parents to come here in the first place. For me to be dating a Farcliff Prince? That might be a little much for them to take in."

I resist the urge to put my hand to my stomach. Every second sentence, I think of telling him about the baby, but the words just won't come out.

It's been nice having him here. It's been comforting knowing that my pillow smells like him, and that his shoes are lined up beside mine by the front door.

If I tell him now, it'll ruin everything. The past few weeks have been so, so good, and I just... I can't bring myself to say the words that will end it all.

Damon wraps his arms around my waist and rests his chin on top of my head. I nuzzle into his chest and listen to his heartbeat. I'm stuck in limbo, torn between enjoying his company and telling him the truth. I know that once I tell him about the baby, everything will change.

"We're going to have to tell people that we're together eventually."

"I know," I say.

His arms tighten around me and I take a deep, shuddering breath. My world is falling to pieces around me, and all I'm doing is standing here, watching it happen.

Right now, Prince Damon and I are in a safe little cocoon. No one knows that we've been seeing each other—not even Elle. Our relationship has been loving and tender and perfect. We've spent every night with each other, and text each other throughout the day. He hasn't needed to self-harm, and I haven't worried about being cursed.

But now...

...everything is different. It's all going to end.

It would be enough of a controversy for one of the Princes of Farcliff to be dating a Raventhal—but to have a baby with me? An *illegitimate* baby with me?

Scandal-city. Tabloid central. The end of Farcliff as we know it.

Worry knots my stomach. The Prince cups my cheek and presses his lips to mine.

"We'll figure this out, Dahlia."

I nod, not believing a word.

"You do want to be with me, right?" His eyebrows arch and his eyes look so clear and sincere that my heart aches.

"Of course I want to be with you." I choke on the last

word as emotion clouds my eyes. I try to fill my lungs up, but it's hard to take a full breath. I want nothing more than to be with him! Being with him has been like finally taking a breath of air after being stuck underwater. It's like seeing the sun after being underground for months. It's like waking up after a bad dream.

Being with Damon is everything I never knew I wanted, and it's all going to change the minute I tell him the truth.

"Look, if you don't want to go public with me yet, I understand that. I saw how the media swarmed my brother and Elle. We're both busy with school and work, and I know that everything will change once people know we're together." Damon tightens his arm around me.

"It's just so perfect now," I whisper. "I don't want to ruin it—*us*."

"Nothing can ruin us," Damon says as he kisses me again. "I won't let it happen. I promise."

I nod and force a smile, but the sick feeling in my stomach gets stronger and I know that's a promise that Damon can't possibly keep.

Damon's hands slide down to my ass, and I tilt my head up to look at him. He's still the most handsome man I've ever seen. He still makes my pulse quicken. I still want him more than I can explain.

So, for a little bit longer, I want to stay in this cocoon of ours. When I figure out the right words to use to tell him about the baby, then I'll say them. For now, though, I just press my lips to his and enjoy the warmth of his embrace.

# 26

# DAMON

I MOVE BACK to the castle after my shift at the Farcliff General Hospital. As far as I can tell, no one even noticed I was gone.

It's okay. I usually keep to myself, anyway. I have no staff, and I spend most of my days studying. Being out of sight for a few weeks wouldn't be unheard of, so the past couple of weeks at Dahlia's house didn't raise anyone's attention. The entire castle was too busy preparing for the baby to notice anything about me.

Wandering over to our private sitting room, where guests are usually received, I find my brothers with Elle, Dahlia, and her parents.

All eyes turn to me when I walk in. Dahlia's face brightens, but she stays seated where she is, beside Elle and the baby Prince.

Mr. and Mrs. Raventhal are different from what I'd expected. They're somber, serious people—nothing like Dahlia. Mrs. Raventhal's face is creased and aged beyond her years, as if she's been wracked with stress her entire life.

She has Farcliff to blame for that, I suppose.

"Damon," King Charlie says, standing. Everyone else in

the room stands as he does. "Nice of you to join us. I'd like to introduce you to Mr. and Mrs. Raventhal. We were just talking about how thrilled we are to have them back in Farcliff."

Introductions are made all around. I take a seat in a chair across from Dahlia. Her eyes dart up to meet mine and a blush creeps over her cheeks.

I hadn't anticipated that I might actually enjoy being at the castle with her—that I might like sneaking around.

Dahlia crosses one leg over the other, and my eyes follow the movement, my mouth salivating at the thought spreading those legs wide.

How does she do this to me?

I can be in a room full of people—including her parents—and Dahlia still turns me on like crazy. She doesn't even realize she's doing it.

I put on my best polite smile and try to act like a normal person in a normal social situation, even though all I can think about is getting Dahlia and her pink-tipped hair back to my chambers. We haven't had sex in days and there's been weird distance between us.

Maybe being at the castle is exactly what we need—a change of scenery. A new bed.

When she looks my way again, I try to motion toward the door. Her lips twitch, and I know she understands. I stand up, take my leave, and then slip out through the door.

My heart thumps. I practically run down the hallway toward my chambers. My hands tremble as I reach into my pocket for my phone so I can tell Dahlia where I'm going. My blood is flowing hot through my veins, and the anticipation is making my vision tunnel.

I'm already thinking about her lily-white body splayed out on my bed, her hands twisting into my silk sheets, her screams muffled in my down pillows. Having her here in the castle makes me think about our first evening together, when I broke every single castle rule with her in the throne room.

Yes—being here with Dahlia is a very, very good idea.

They say that texting while walking accounts for at least fifty percent of all pedestrian deaths in Farcliff, and as I turn the corner, I understand why. I walk head-first into another body, jumping back in surprise as we both stumble backward.

"Aunt Malerie!"

"Nephew." She brushes imaginary dust off her dress. "Where are you going so quickly?"

"Back to my room," I say, slipping my phone back into my pocket after I hit the 'send' button.

My aunt's eyes don't miss anything. She watches the movement and then flicks her gaze back to my face. Her eyebrow arches, and she takes a step toward me.

"We're not so different, you and I," she purrs.

*Maybe, but at least I don't smell like onions.*

"Oh yeah?" I ask, trying my best to sound casual. Three seconds ago, I was thinking of burying my face between Dahlia's legs, and now my aunt wants to catch up like we're old friends.

Great.

"Well, we're both second in line for the throne. Both destined to be forgotten in the history books. Both not quite good enough to wear the Crown."

"I don't want the Crown." My brows draw together and I glance over my shoulder. I don't want Dahlia to walk up to us now.

"Maybe you think that today, but you'll watch your brother lap up the adulation of the people, and resentment will fester." Mal's eyes darken and her lips twist downward.

"You might not feel it yet, but being in second place for your entire life does tend to wear a person down."

Is this why she's always so easily offended? Why she's on edge all the time? Plain, old-fashioned *jealousy*?

I shake my head. "Aunt Mal, I'm telling the truth. I don't even stay at the castle most days. I'm giving up my royal title to go to med school. I don't *want* the Crown."

Her head tilts. "If you don't stay at the castle, where do you stay?"

Something in the way she asks the question makes fear spark in the pit of my stomach. The hair on my arm stands on end, and I try my hardest to keep my breath steady.

I gulp, averting my eyes and shrugging. "I have an apartment in town," I lie. I don't want to tell my aunt where I've been staying. I've already seen the way she looks at Dahlia, and I don't like it. I don't want to give Aunt Mal an excuse to hate her—or an excuse for Dahlia to fear my family any more than she already does.

My aunt stares at me for a few more seconds, and then takes a deep breath and seems to relax.

"Did you know the name Malerie comes from the French word *malheur*? It literally means 'unlucky'." My aunt shakes her head, sighing. "It's all too appropriate."

"No, I didn't know that." I glance up and down the hallway, ready for this conversation to be over. I don't like talking to my aunt at the best of times, and this is just getting fucking weird.

"You and I should go to lunch one day, nephew. We have more in common than you think."

"Does my name mean 'unlucky', too?"

Malerie just laughs, and another wave of onion wafts toward me. I smile awkwardly and try to motion around her. I already texted Dahlia, and I need to get back to my chambers to meet her. Given the option between standing in a hallway having an awkward conversation with my half-estranged aunt, or taking my girlfriend back to my bed and fucking her brains out, I know which one I'd choose.

It isn't my aunt.

Before I can move past her, though, her eyes brighten and a cruel smile stretches across her lips.

"Well, well, well," she says, staring past me.

I feel Dahlia's hand on my arm before I even turn around to look, and my heart sinks. Dahlia is trembling. Her eyes are wide as she looks up at my aunt. She curtsies delicately, and then glances up at me.

Malerie grins at the two of us. "Is this the apartment in town that you were talking about?"

"Nice to see you, Aunt, but if you'll excuse me..."

I step around her, giving her a wide berth. She just keeps grinning at Dahlia and I as we shuffle past, and then half-jog down the hallway until she's out of view.

"What was that about?" Dahlia whispers when we're a safe distance away. Her hand floats to her stomach almost protectively. The movement looks familiar, but I can't quite place where I've seen it before. Dahlia's eyebrows draw together.

"I'm not sure. I didn't even know she was in the castle. I thought she left the day of the wedding."

"She gives me the creeps."

"Me too." I put my hand around Dahlia's shoulders and hold her tight. We make it to my chambers without seeing anyone else, and I lock the door with a sigh.

Dahlia is twisting the fabric of her dress between her hands. She stares at the floor, chewing her bottom lip until I take her hands and place them around my neck.

"Don't worry about my kooky old aunt," I say gently. "You're safe with me."

Dahlia takes a deep breath and forces a smile. "Yeah," she says. "Okay. What did she want, anyway?"

I wave my hand dismissively, shaking my head. "She kept saying that she and I were the same, second in line for the throne and always destined to be disappointed."

"Huh." Dahlia frowns.

"I kept telling her that I didn't want the Crown. I want my own life—because you know, *a king is history's slave.*"

Dahlia's eyes brighten and a delighted laugh tumbles through her lips. "Tolstoy!"

I grin and pull her closer to me. "I've been waiting for an opportunity to use that. It was the only quote that was short enough for me to remember."

Dahlia just laughs and lays a soft kiss on my lips. The tension between us eases, and she melts into my arms. Feeling her like this makes me feel like everything will be okay. We'll get over this stupid family feud. We'll be together. Everything will be fine.

We lay in bed together, but instead of the crazy, feral sex I'd envisioned, all I do is hold her. I wrap my arms around her as she puts her head to my chest, drawing small circles with her finger. I stroke her hair and kiss her forehead, loving the way she feels in my arms.

As much as she struggles to believe me, I know I'd do anything to keep her safe—from what, though, I'm not exactly sure. I just know that whatever Dahlia is worried about—whatever fears are on her mind—I'll be right there with her to face them.

# 27

## DAHLIA

SEEING Damon's aunt in the hallway throws me off. She looks at me like I was a fawn in the forest, and she was a hungry wolf.

But Damon holds me until I felt okay again, and then we make love. When it's over, I look around the rich, ornate furnishings and I wonder if I really belong here. My mother does—she looked at home in the formal living room, perched on the edge of an expensive chaise. My father looked equally as comfortable, eating the rich food and drinking the fine wine that was offered to him.

I'm not so sure. I may be their daughter, but I grew up living a simple life.

Tiptoeing out of Damon's room at around midnight, I make my way through the silent corridors back to my own guest bedroom. It takes me nearly twenty minutes to get there, because I make a couple wrong turns and end up in the opposite wing of the palace. It's eerily quiet at night here.

When I finally find my way back to my own room, I climb into bed and breathe a sigh of relief. My ears ring in the silence, and I try to hear a noise—any noise—that might help me fall asleep. At home, there's always the sound of cars on the road, or the creaking of the house in the wind. Sometimes, I can even hear the scratching of mice in the walls.

Here in the castle, there's nothing. You'd think it would be easier to sleep when it's quiet, but there's nothing to drown out my racing thoughts.

I finally do get to sleep, though. When I wake up to the sun streaming through the sheer curtains, with a tray of fresh coffee on my nightstand and warm slippers ready for me to wear, my attitude toward castle life improves quite a bit.

Staying at the castle isn't that bad. Dare I say—it's actually *nice*. It's much closer to the Farcliff University campus, so my commute to classes and to the lab is almost halved. As much as I teased Damon about his feather beds, it *is* nice to have a decent mattress.

After a couple of nights, I even get used to the absolute silence of the night.

My parents stay at the castle longer than expected. The King and Queen are gracious and welcoming, and I watch my parents relax into their old life at the castle. We spend the holidays here as a family. Even my aunts make it to the castle for Christmas dinner.

It's nice. It feels more and more homey. I try not to think about the baby—I think I'm in denial. Maybe I'm too weak, or too scared, but I don't want to ruin what I have. Damon and I are happy together, my parents are comfortable in Farcliff, and it finally feels like we have a future here.

After five weeks at the palace, I'm almost used to the feather beds and excessive pomp and circumstance of literally everything. Breakfast is a whole ordeal with silver trays, butlers, and a banquet table loaded with rich foods.

In January, classes start again. I stare at myself in the mirror every morning, wondering if my bump is starting to show. I'm two months pregnant, and I still haven't told a soul.

Call me weak. Call me a coward. Call me whatever you want—I've already called myself worse. For the first time in my life, I get to be with my parents and see them happy. I have a man that I care about—and maybe even love. He cares about me, too.

I don't want to ruin it. For a few more days, or maybe a couple of more weeks, I just want to cling on to this feeling.

I'll tell them. I will. Just—not right now.


"Well, they sure do know how to cater," my father says with a wink one morning.

I slather some crunchy peanut butter on a piece of toast and grin at him. "They sure do."

I glance over at my mother, who seems to have relaxed a bit. She even has a smile on her face as she sips her morning coffee.

King Charlie enters the room with Elle and their baby. We all stand. Elle glances at me and rolls her eyes—she's obviously still not used to all this rigamarole. I grin. She's still the same old Elle. I watch her with her baby, and my heart squeezes.

She's the same old Elle, with a baby and a husband and a happy life. Maybe that's possible for me, too?

Damon is still working nights, so I still don't get to see much of him. He won't be back at the castle for another couple of hours, and by that time, I'll be in class. It's okay, though. We steal whatever moments we can and always make the most of our time together.

"How did you sleep, Mother?" I ask, taking a seat next to my mom.

When she turns to look at me, her eyes are clear and she seems to have fewer lines on her face.

"I slept wonderfully, Dahlia." She takes another sip of coffee and lets out a satisfied sigh.

I glance around the room at our little family—because Elle and Charlie are family, too—and hope sparks in my heart. Maybe Damon is right. With Charlie and Elle on the throne, things will change. Maybe, before my parents leave Farcliff again, I can tell them that I've been dating him.

Maybe when I tell him about the baby, things won't fall apart. Maybe I can get my own happily ever after, too.

*Maybe, maybe, maybe...*

I finish my breakfast and a castle worker whisks my plate away. The movement startles me—just as it always does.

Except this time, I don't spill my coffee, or flip a plate over, or fall on the floor. Nothing bad happens. He just takes my plate away. There's no curse, no clumsiness—nothing. A grin touches my lips, and hope burns brighter in my heart.

It might be silly, but even being less clumsy makes me think that things might just work out. It's like it's a sign from the Universe telling me that things are looking up.

"Oh, Dahlia." Elle—or, Queen Elle, as she's now known— stands up to stop me. She puts her hand on Charlie's shoulder and a smile drifts over her lips.

"What is it?"

"Well," Elle glances from me to my parents. "Since we're all here, I was hoping to ask you something." Her eyes are shining. Charlie reaches up to squeeze her hand as it rests on his shoulder.

"Okay."

Elle takes a deep breath. "Would you be Charlie's

godmother? The christening is next week. You've been there for both Charlie and me for a long time, and I can't think of anyone better."

My mother's face breaks into a smile and my heart skips a beat. I suck in a breath, and the room stills.

This feels significant. My mother was named Charlie's godmother, before everything went to shit. Before the murder of the Queen, before the exile, before our family name was dirt.

Elle's eyes widen and she stares at me expectantly.

Maybe this is a way to make up for the past. Maybe this time around, we can do things right. Naming me godmother would send a very clear message about the Raventhal name, and what it means in Farcliff. We wouldn't be the butt of bad jokes anymore. I wouldn't have to hide who I really am.

I'd be the Crown Prince's godmother. My own mother would be redeemed, and we could all move on with our lives.

I could tell Damon about the baby without being afraid that I'd be thrown out or disgraced.

"Well?" Elle says softly.

I nod, smiling. "Of course, Elle—er, Your Majesty. I'd be honored."

"Don't you start calling me Your Majesty," she laughs, striding toward me. She wraps me in a tight hug, squeezing me to her breast. "Thank you, Dahlia."

"Thank *you*, and you, Charlie."

The King smiles. "Wouldn't have it any other way."

I glance at my mother and father, who both nod at me gently. Their demeanor has changed over the past week. They're no longer wracked with worry. My mother stands up and glides toward me, putting her hands on my shoulders. She smiles at me and kisses my cheek.

"I'm proud of you," she whispers.

My heart flutters. I'm beaming, staring at each of them in turn. I walk over to baby Charlie and kiss his forehead. Then, I straighten up and take a deep breath.

"I'm going to be late for class."

Elle grins at me, and nods as if to say I can go. Within just a couple of months, she's already become regal.

I slip out of the door and float all the way to campus. Being the Prince's godmother is an incredible honor, and my heart is soaring.

After my mother's reaction to that news, I know that I can tell her about Damon and me. I know that my mother is beginning to overcome her fear of Farcliff, and there's a real chance she'll approve of me dating one of the princes...

...and if I can tell my parents about my relationship, maybe I can tell Damon about the baby, too.

I make it through the whole day of classes with a smile on my face, and then make my way to the lab for work. When I walk in, I'm not afraid of breaking the glass instruments or tripping over some expensive equipment. I feel confident, and comfortable, and most importantly, I feel like everything might just turn out alright.

# 28

# DAMON

My residency is becoming more like an endurance marathon than a learning experience. Nights are long and slow, and the tiredness seeps into my bones. Even day shifts are grueling.

I haven't been seeing much of Dahlia, but we spend every minute we can together. Even when I'm off, I spend my time reading, studying, and doing paperwork. She studies alongside me, and my love for her grows every day.

I never thought I'd say that word—love. But it's there, simmering just under the surface. It's budding in my heart, slowly pushing out the darkness that resided there before.

Tonight, I'm midway through my ICU rotation. It's a busy night. There are a few incidents in Grimdale, including a couple of gunshot wounds that my shift has to deal with.

In the moment, when the patients come in, I'm focused, clear-headed and ready to do the work. As soon as it's over, though, I find a quiet supply closet in the hospital and sink down onto the floor.

Dropping my head in my hands, I take a few deep, raking breaths.

Not for the first time, I wonder if this is really what I want to do. I'm giving up a life of luxury for this. I've worked hard for years to get to where I am, but now that I'm here, I'm not so sure it's what I really want to do.

Why did I go into medicine in the first place?

I don't even know what time it is. The hospital is like a time warp. Leaning my head against the steel shelves stacked with cleaning products, I pull my phone out of my pocket to see a message from Dahlia.

**Dahlia: I have some good news :)**

A smile stretches over my face and my heart beats a little easier.

**Damon: What is it?**

**Dahlia: I'll tell you when I see you.**

I grin. Dahlia lifts my mood every single time I talk to her—even if it's only a short text. I slip my phone back into my pocket and heave myself up to my feet. My legs are sore and my feet are aching. I rub my palms over my face and take a deep breath before pushing the door open again.

My attending physician is at the end of the hospital. She waves at me. "Come on. We've got another one."

I END up sleeping on one of the couches in the staff lounge for two or three hours, and then having to get up for my next shift.

It's grueling, but when I drag my feet to the cafeteria and shovel down some food before I start work, I don't feel as despondent as I did this morning. This is what I want to do.

Yes, I'm giving up a lot to do it, but it's my calling. I want to help people—even if it means working long hours.

I'm tired, but I'm happy.

I text Dahlia again around dinnertime, telling her that I probably won't be at the castle for at least another day. If the hospital is as busy tonight as it was last night, I'm not sure when I'll see the outside world again.

My phone rings a couple minutes later.

"Hey," she says. "Stuck at the hospital?"

"Yeah." I'm sitting in the cafeteria, watching the other doctors, nurses, and hospital staff shuffle from one side of the room to the other. Everyone looks tired.

I take a deep breath. "What was this big news? I don't think I can wait a whole other day."

Dahlia laughs, and the sound soothes my soul. I don't know what I did before her—everything is easier with her in my life. A smile drifts over my lips, and I let out a sigh.

"Well," she says slowly, savoring the drama of the moment. "Charlie and Elle asked me to be little Charlie's godmother!"

I smile, leaning my head in my hand as I listen to her. Dahlia's voice is full of life and love, and it gives me strength.

"That's great," I say. "I wonder who they'll choose as the godfather."

"I was thinking that maybe we should tell them we've been seeing each other."

I straighten up, my eyebrows arching in surprise. "Yeah?"

"Yeah. I mean, it's been a couple of months and nothing disastrous has happened." She laughs and I can imagine her scrunching her nose. "My parents seem really happy to be back in Farcliff. I think it might be a good time to tell them about us."

"I agree," I say. I've been waiting for this. As much fun as sneaking around is, what I really want is for everyone to know that Dahlia is mine—and I'm hers.

I want to scream it from the rooftops. I want a royal decree sent out to every house in Farcliff, declaring my love for her to the whole Kingdom.

Dahlia lets out a long sigh. "Thank you for being patient with me."

"It was easy."

"Still," she says. "I appreciate it."

"I'd better go. My shift is starting soon and I have to take a quick shower. I'll see you tomorrow, okay?"

"Yeah. Hey, Damon?"

"Uh huh?"

"I... I'm proud of you."

My heart skips a beat and I swallow past a lump in my throat. For a second, I thought she was going to tell me she loved me.

The fact that she's ready to tell our families about us is almost as good.

"I'm proud of you, too. Have fun staring into your microscope tonight."

She laughs. "Trust me, I will."

"See you tomorrow." I hang up the phone and take a deep breath. My lips tug up into a smile and I lean back in my chair, savoring these last moments of calm before my shift.

This period of my life—with medical residency, the controversy with my father, and my relationship with Dahlia—has been the most chaotic time I've ever experienced, but it's also been the most rewarding. I can't help but feel like I'm heading in the right direction, and that once we make it through this, everything might just work out.

# 29

# DAHLIA

I HANG up the phone with Damon and bask in the happiness of the moment. Things are going to work out—I know they will.

Before Damon and I tell our friends and family we're together, I'm going to tell him about the baby. I make a vow to myself that the next time I see him, I'll sit him down and say it to him.

It's the right thing to do—it's been too long already. He deserves to know.

Whatever happens after that, happens. I need to trust that he cares about me, and that he'll care about this baby. I can already feel my love for the child growing, and carrying it on my own is becoming difficult. With my parents here, and being named godmother, it seems like as good a time as ever.

I spend a couple of hours in the lab. By the time I make it back to the castle, the sun is starting to set. Texting Elle to see where she is, I find her in a sunroom at the back of the castle.

She lifts her head when I walk up to her. Baby Charlie is in his stroller, asleep.

"Hi," she smiles. She looks exhausted, but happy.

"Hey," I say, sitting down on the bench next to her. I glance around the sunroom, and at the winter scene in front of us, and I sigh. "It's nice back here."

"I'm still finding so many new corners in the castle that I didn't know existed," she smiles. "I don't know if I'll ever see it all."

"I'm sure you will."

"It's been nice having you here," Elle says, glancing at me. "It makes the castle feel like home."

"I never thought I'd say it, but I agree," I laugh. "I actually feel good being here."

"Your parents seem to have adjusted."

"They're happy. Thank you for welcoming them back."

Elle shakes her head. "It was a no-brainer."

"Any news on the investigation into the Queen's death?"

"Charlie doesn't tell me much," Elle sighs. "With the baby being born, I haven't really asked. I know it's hard on him."

I nod.

"We know that the Queen was murdered, and we know that the former King was involved," Elle says. "Beyond that, not much."

"What about Malerie Farcliff?"

Elle sighs, shaking her head. "No proof of involvement. She was out of the Kingdom at the time."

"She makes me uncomfortable."

"She's strange," Elle agrees.

I open my mouth to say something, but I'm interrupted by the sunroom door opening. Malerie Farcliff steps through as if summoned by the sound of her own name.

She glances at us and gives Elle the slightest of curtsies. Elle inclines her head. Their greeting is as frosty as the January weather outside.

"Cold day to be in the gardens," Elle remarks.

"I was checking on the honeybees after last week's cold snap," Malerie says, shaking the snow off her shoulders.

I frown. "I thought bees hibernated."

"Not honeybees," Lady Malerie says, pinching her lips. "That's why they make honey—to survive the winter."

"Huh." I nod. "I didn't know that."

"I brought those bees back from Yemen over a decade ago," Lady Malerie says, leaning over the stroller to stroke baby Charlie's cheek. Elle stiffens beside me. "That's why Farcliff honey is renowned now."

"Oh, Prince Damon told me that," I say, remembering my first evening at the castle.

Malerie takes a hand and pushes her sleek, waist-length hair over her shoulder and narrows her eyes at me. "You've been spending lots of time with my nephew."

An uneasy silence falls between us. I clear my throat. "Beekeeping is something I'd love to get into, but I can't."

"No?" Lady Malerie says, arching an eyebrow. She shrugs her jacket off and a single bee buzzes out from the sleeve. So she was telling the truth—they don't hibernate.

I freeze, watching it.

"No, I'm allergic." My pulse quickens the tiniest bit. I have my EpiPen in my bag, don't I?

"How unfortunate," she says, holding out her hand. "Honeybees are some of the loveliest creatures on the planet."

The insect lands on her finger and starts crawling over the back of her hand. She twists her hand over and cups the bee in her palm. Lady Malerie watches it, and then lifts her eyes to me.

"I believe congratulations are in order." Her eyes flick to my stomach, and my blood turns to ice. "You're going to be little Charlie's godmother."

Relief floods through me. I thought she knew about the baby. Having Malerie Farcliff spill the beans to Elle was *not* how I'd envisioned telling everyone.

I nod, keeping my eyes on the insect she's holding in her hand. My pulse is hammering, and my mouth has gone dry. Did she not hear me when I said I was allergic?

I don't mean slightly allergic—I'm not talking a few hives and a swollen throat. I mean I'm anaphylactic. That bee could kill me...

...and my baby.

My hand flies to my stomach, and Malerie's eyes widen. Her gaze flicks up to my face, and anger blazes in her eyes.

*She knows.*

"Lady Malerie, if you wouldn't mind taking that bee outside," Elle says, pulling the baby to her breast. "Dahlia is allergic and I'd rather not have it so close to the baby."

"I'd better get going, anyway," I say, stammering. I stand up and nod to the two women before turning toward the door.

I've only taken one step when I hear Malerie say a soft 'oh'.

A moment later there's a sharp prick on my finger. Bringing my hand up, I see a bead of blood on the tip of my finger. I frown, staring at it.

What could possibly...?

Then, the dizziness hits. My throat feels itchy and breathing becomes difficult. Still, I don't understand. I turn slowly toward the two women, still staring at my finger.

Movement on the ground catches my eye.

The bee, writhing around on the floor.

Confusion turns to horror as I stare at my finger again. I try to say something, but no sound comes out. My hand flies to my throat as I try to take a breath. I wheeze, clawing at my neck.

Elle says something panicked. I can't make out the words. I try to breathe in again, but nothing can make it through. Falling to my knees, I scratch my throat as if that will help me inhale. I can't see. I can't breathe. I'm drowning even though there's no water.

I don't have my EpiPen—why would I? It's winter. I collapse onto my side as the dizziness becomes too much. The room is spinning and I can't think.

Elle screams. I hear the thumping of boots.

My vision goes black, and I'm gone.

# 30

# DAMON

I STUMBLE home after more than fifty hours at the hospital and collapse straight into bed. I haven't heard from Dahlia all day, but I'm too tired to message her. I'm too tired to talk to anyone.

At least I'm on the day shift now.

One good thing about residency is that the exhaustion lends itself to amazing sleep. I don't have time to think, or worry, or do anything except shovel some food into my mouth and pass out.

When I wake up again, after only a few short hours, I drag myself out of bed and take a quick shower. I need to be back at the hospital for another shift in less than an hour.

Everything is always rushed, and I don't have time to think about much. It's been almost a full day since I heard from Dahlia, so I send her a message to make sure she's okay. When I walk out of my bedroom and make my way to the garage, the castle is eerily quiet.

Worry tickles the base of my skull. Something doesn't feel right—but, then again, I haven't slept more than four hours a night for over two weeks, so how would I know what feels right and what doesn't? Everything feels like a dream these days.

I hear some heated voices in one of the living rooms, but I don't have time to stop. I make it to my car and drive back to the hospital.

My shift starts as normal. After a handover from the night shift, I start making my rounds. It's quieter than it has been all week, and for once the emergency department isn't overrun. After a few hours, Dr. Adler calls out to me.

"Farcliff!"

I turn to see my attending physician striding down the hall. She waves me toward her. When I reach her, Dr. Adler's eyes are bright. She nods down the hall.

"Farcliff Royal had a really interesting case come in last night. It's an incredible learning opportunity, and I think it's worth going over there. We've got enough cover here before the afternoon rounds. Come on."

My attending motions toward the door, and I fall into step with her.

"I'll drive," she says.

"Who's the patient?"

"Young woman, twenty-three years old," she starts. "Came in going into anaphylactic shock. She arrived with the Queen of Farcliff, can you believe that?" Dr. Adler glances at me. "Right—of course you can believe that. I forget who you are sometimes."

Alarm bells start ringing in my head. I touch my phone in my pocket, but it still hasn't buzzed all day. My heart rate increases and I struggle to take a breath.

"So, the patient?"

"Allergic to bees and got stung by one up at the castle. Talk about unlucky. I thought bees hibernated."

Didn't Dahlia say she was allergic to bee stings? Was I imagining that?

Dr. Adler continues. "This way. She's stable now, but was comatose when she made it to the hospital. That's not what's most interesting, though." Her eyes are gleaming, as if she's happy about this. "I'll tell you when we get there."

I feel like I'm going to throw up.

We drive in silence—the other hospital is only a short drive away. Farcliff Royal is another teaching hospital, and we often have patients and residents transfer from one to the other. When we get there, Adler parks in the staff parking lot and leads me toward the Farcliff Royal Hospital's ICU.

Last time I was here was for my nephew's birth. Now…

Adler motions to another hallway and I breathe in through my nose. I need to calm down. It's not Dahlia. It can't be. There are many, many other people at the Farcliff Castle —it's definitely not Dahlia. She's probably in class or something, and that's why she hasn't answered my phone calls. Maybe she's in the lab with her nose stuck in a book.

Yes, she's allergic to bees—but so are other people! She wouldn't have gone anywhere near the hives. It's probably one of the beekeepers or one of the gardeners who got lost.

*She came in with the Queen.*

It's not Dahlia. It can't be.

I keep telling myself these things, trying to keep my panic at bay. My mouth is dry and I flex and unflex my hands as we ride up the elevator. My vision tunnels and I can hardly see straight. Dr. Adler doesn't seem to notice. She's rattling on excitedly. It's the case of a lifetime, apparently.

When the doors ding open, Dr. Adler motions down the hall.

"Now, the interesting thing is that when she first came in, we weren't aware that she was pregnant. We only found that out about six hours ago. That's why I want to show her to you. Obstetrics has seen her, and the baby is fine, even though the mother is in a coma. She's about two months pregnant. Incredible!"

My heart is racing. My vision starts to blur. Pregnant? In a coma? No way. No fucking way.

She's not pregnant. We've been careful. It's not her. I'm swinging between total panic and the certainty it isn't Dahlia in that hospital bed.

We reach the room where the patient is being kept, and I pause just outside the door. Glancing at the whiteboard beside the door, I notice that no one has written the patient's name. Typically, the patient's name is displayed outside the room.

Maybe they do things differently at Farcliff Royal Hospital.

Maybe they do things differently for members of the Farcliff Royal Court—people like Dahlia Raventhal.

I'm going to throw up. Cold sweat is dripping down between my shoulder blades, and my vision is going blurry. I can't face it. I can't go in there.

If it's Dahlia, I don't know what I'll do.

Squeezing my eyes shut, I take a deep breath.

When I open them back up, Dr. Adler is staring at me funnily. "Everything okay?"

"Didn't get much sleep," I answer weakly.

She nods. "Get used to it."

I look at the door and take a deep breath. It'll only take me two steps to walk inside, and then I'll know who the patient is. I'll know if Dahlia is on that hospital bed.

I'll know if she's carrying my child.

My mouth is dry and I clench my hands into fists. I take

the first step, sucking a breath in and strengthening my resolve. I take another step...

...and my stomach bottoms out.

*Dahlia.*

*My* Dahlia. My love.

She's pale. Her eyes are closed and her arms are laying limply by her sides. Machines beep all around her, but I can't hear anything. Dr. Adler's voice fades into the distance and all I can do is stand there and stare.

I want to scream. I want to cry. I want to smash every window in this room and shake Dahlia until she wakes up. My stomach rolls, and I feel like I'm going to vomit.

I can't make any sense of it.

Anaphylaxis. Coma.

*Pregnant.*

My breath is coming in short, ragged bursts. I stumble, catching myself on the wall as I bend over double and try to fill my lungs. I can't get enough oxygen. I can't think straight. I squeeze my eyes shut and put my head between my legs.

Dr. Adler's hand appears on my back and vaguely, I hear her calling for help. She drags a chair over and forces me into it, propping my head up and staring into my eyes. A nurse rushes in and I snap back to the moment.

"Damon!"

"I'm okay," I wheeze. "I'm okay."

"What the fuck just happened?"

"I know..." I'm still panting. I can't get a full breath in. My tongue feels too big for my mouth and I can't string words together properly. I point to the bed. "Dahlia."

"You know the patient?"

I inhale sharply and squeeze my eyes shut, digging my fingernails into my legs to try to get myself together. The pain sharpens my senses and I finally take a full breath.

"I know Dahlia," I say. "I'm the father."

Dr. Adler's eyes widen. She stumbles backward, staring at me as if I've just sprouted another head. I swing my eyes over to Dahlia's bed, and panic starts to rise in my throat again.

Then, someone clears their throat in the doorway. My heart sinks even lower when I see Mr. and Mrs. Raventhal staring at me with the same expression Dr. Adler has on her face.

I struggle to my feet, opening my mouth to say something—anything. I want to apologize, but what am I apologizing for? I want to tell them I love her—I've loved her for months, but how will they believe me? I want to tell them I care about her, and I'll do anything to bring her back...

...but before any words make it out of my mouth, Tabitha Raventhal strides toward me and slaps me clean across the face.

# 31

## DAMON

I'M PUSHED out of the hospital room by the other staff. Stumbling, I catch myself on the hallway wall and gulp down a breath. Dr. Adler leaves the room to speak with me.

"If I'd had any idea..."

"It's not your fault," I say. "No one could have known."

"Well... Congratulations?" Dr. Adler's eyebrows shoot up as she says the word. She cringes, and I scoff.

"Thanks."

I can feel the dark rot poisoning my blood already. Glancing back toward Dahlia's room, it feels like my heart is turning black in my chest.

How could she have a bee sting in January? How could this happen?

*How could she be pregnant?*

I bring my hand to my forehead and let out a long breath. This isn't right. None of this is right. My thoughts swirl around me like a black cloud, and I can't make sense of any of them—except that Dahlia is lying limp in that hospital bed.

"How many hours did you say she'd been in a coma?" I ask.

Dr. Adler checks her watch. "She came in at about eight o'clock last night, so sixteen hours now."

I nod. "And the baby?"

"The baby's okay, for now." She puts her hand on my arm. "There have been cases of women giving birth while in a coma."

"Giving birth in a coma?" Panic laces every word.

Dr. Adler takes a deep breath. "I'm just saying, it can happen. The sooner she wakes up, the better for them both. You know as well as I do—the longer she stays in a coma, the more dangerous things become. We don't know if she'll wake up—or in what state she'll wake up in. We'll try to get her out of it, but for now all we can do is hope."

I shake my head.

All we can do is hope? *Hope?*

With all the years and years of medical research, the best we can do is fucking *hope?*

I've spent the better part of the last decade studying every bit of the human body, and now all I can do is hang my life on a prayer?

Is this a fucking joke?

Tabitha Raventhal appears in Dahlia's doorway. Her eyes are dark, and deep lines are back on her face. She stares me down and then closes the door firmly. It latches shut, and the sound pierces my heart like a dagger.

I'm trying my best to keep it together, but I'm falling apart. Every part of my body is trembling and it's all I can do to breathe.

Dr. Adler puts her hand on my arm and leads me down the hallway. "You should go home," she says softly.

"Why didn't she tell me?"

I'm not really asking Dr. Adler. She won't have an answer.

Plus, I already know why Dahlia didn't tell me about the

baby. The answer to that question happened right here in this hospital, the day that baby Charlie was born. I saw it in her face when I told her I didn't want kids.

She was pregnant then, and I told her I didn't want it. I said it right to her face.

How could I be so stupid? How could I say something like that? Of course I want the child. Of course I want to be with her. These have been the happiest months of my life, but I told her I didn't want a future with her.

The darkness starts to overwhelm me. My fingers are tingling, and I'm starting to lose feeling in my feet. I stumble over the floor, and Dr. Adler catches me.

"Go home, Damon. Is there someone who can pick you up?"

"I don't want to go home."

Where is home, anyway? The castle? Every part of that castle reminds me of Dahlia. My bed, her bed, the throne room, the dining room, the solarium, my study—every single room is burned into my memory with her.

Maybe I could go to her house in Grimdale.

I snort at the thought. Yeah, right. She's infused into the very fabric of that house. How can I go back there without wanting to tear my own skin off?

I pace the hallway until Dr. Adler leads me to the foyer of the hospital.

In the end, one of the royal cars comes to take me back to the castle. I pinch my lips shut and say nothing to anyone, dragging my feet up to my chambers and locking the door.

I check the time—1:30pm. She's been in a coma for seventeen and a half hours. I lay in bed and twist my hands into the bedsheets, trying to take a deep breath.

I know this feeling. I haven't felt it in months—not once since Dahlia and I have been together. It's overwhelming—

the blackness, the hurt, the torture in my own mind. I'm eating myself from the inside out. My whole body is in pain, but not the kind of pain I can latch onto.

Nigel could help me. I could spend the night on a dirty cot and wake up with sweet, painful bruises all over my body. I could bleed for her.

But then, I remember her face when she asked me to stop going to the warehouse. The way her eyebrows drew together, and the sadness in her eyes. I remember the way she kissed me and melted into my arms.

I resist.

I don't deserve to let go of this feeling. I don't deserve the release.

So, I just lie there and suffer.

THE HOURS TICK BY, second by second, eternity by eternity. I replay every moment I've had with Dahlia, wishing I could go back and change something.

Why didn't she tell me? Why didn't she trust me?

I should have told her I loved her. I've loved her for months, but I was too chicken to tell her. I should have held her tight and told her I loved her every single day.

What if I never get the chance?

After eight hours, I get out of bed. My stomach is in knots, and I feel like I've just done a thirty-hour shift. In reality, though, I've just been lying in bed, catatonic.

Making my way back to the hospital, my stomach is in my throat. Someone would have called if Dahlia had woken up.

They would have called if something bad had happened.

Still, when I ride the elevator up to Dahlia's floor, I'm nervous. I lean against the wall to hold myself upright, slinking down the corridor toward her room.

I glance at the clock and count the hours since she was brought in.

Twenty-two hours. Every hour feels like a year. Every second feels like a lifetime. And still, Dahlia sleeps.

Is the baby okay? Is she okay?

My breath becomes ragged and I take a moment to compose myself. When I reach her room, the door is closed. There's a window into her room, and I peek through the edge of it. Dahlia's mother is sitting beside her bed, her forehead resting on the edge of the mattress. She's holding Dahlia's hand in both of hers.

Dahlia is still laying in the same position.

Still limp.

Still comatose.

I die all over again.

I don't need Tabitha Raventhal to hate me—I already hate myself. I don't need her to torture me with guilt—I'm already doing that to myself.

Finding the nearest staff room, I slump down into a chair and put my head in my hands. No one talks to me, and I'm glad.

When I can't sit any longer, I wander the hospital hallways. I pace for another three hours, until I feel like my head is going to explode. Dahlia's condition doesn't change. I sleep on a couch in the residents' staff room for three or four hours, and then I walk the hallways once again. It's not the hospital where I've been working, but the staff let me stay there anyway.

Dahlia's parents don't leave her side. I peek in through the window and I ask the nurses for updates.

No change.

*All we can do is hope.*

Easy for Dr. Adler to say—but when I'm walking back and

forth through the hospital, trying to think of every possible time that I could have avoided this situation, hope is very hard to come by.

I swing by Dahlia's house in Grimdale, and I sleep in our bed for a few hours. I find some scraps to eat, and I let myself sink into a deep, dark hole.

Dahlia's condition doesn't change.

Every minute drags on, and on, and on. I count the hours and pray that she wakes up, but she doesn't. Another day and night passes. I don't even know how I spend it. I ball my hands into fists so tight that my nails slice my palms open. I pull at my hair until a small bald patch appears at the back of my head.

But for all my pain, all my suffering, all my hoping and praying... Dahlia doesn't wake up.

Is it day, or night? I don't even know anymore. I struggle to see straight, and look at the clock for the millionth time. Every minute that goes by is more dangerous for Dahlia— and for the baby.

If she doesn't wake up soon, I'll lose Dahlia just like I lost my mother—silently, in a bed, with nothing I can do to help. With only myself to blame.

The sun starts to go down on the third day, and still, Dahlia sleeps. Still, her parents guard her room and I can't see her. Still, I wander the hospital, the city, the castle.

The night is dark, and I live somewhere between life and death. When the sun starts to come up, I allow myself to hope as I make my way to the hospital again.

The eightieth hour ticks over, and Dahlia doesn't wake up. My heart dies.

# 32

# DAMON

CHARLIE CALLS me and asks me to come back to the castle. He sounds like the King already, commanding and authoritative, and I know I can't refuse him.

With one last look at Dahlia's room, I leave the hospital. It's midday. My entire life has been reduced to watching the clock. The danger for Dahlia increases with every passing hour, and all I can do is wait.

If I thought going to the warehouse and getting the shit kicked out of me was painful, I had no idea.

This, right here—waiting for Dahlia to wake up and being completely powerless to help—this is real pain. This is torture. This is never-ending suffering.

Charlie and Gabe are waiting for me in the King's personal offices. I look around the room, taking note of all the changes Charlie's made since he's been King. He's replaced some of the artwork, and moved the furniture around, but I still see my father's influence in the room.

"Damon," Charlie says gravely. "Thanks for coming."

Gabe's hair is mussed, and he nods to me. "Sorry about Dahlia."

I grunt in response. I guess everyone knows about us being together, and about the baby. At least it means I don't have to tell them. I slump down in a chair, and my whole body aches. I've slept in snippets over the past three and a half days—if you could call it sleep. It's more of an exhausted daze.

Charlie's sitting behind his desk with his hands laced in front of him. He pinches his lips.

"As you know, we exhumed Mother's remains late last year. Her autopsy is complete. I have the results here."

My stomach clenches. I don't know if I have the energy for this. I drop my head in my hands and sit still. Hearing of my mother's death only makes Dahlia's condition more excruciating. How will I handle it if I lose them both?

Charlie takes a deep breath. "Mom died of arsenic poisoning."

"What?" I lift my head up, frowning.

Charlie nods. "They tested her hair."

"How did we not know this before?" Gabe demands. "Are we living in the fucking 1800s? Who poisons people with arsenic?"

"You know who," Charlie says darkly. His eyebrows draw together and he shakes his head. "Father must have had the tests suppressed, or not performed at all. You both know how chaotic that time was."

I can't breathe. I can't think.

Poisoned?

Gabe snorts. "I was four. I don't know how chaotic it was. I barely remember anything. Damon was eight. How the fuck are we supposed to..." His voice trails off and he shakes his head.

Charlie takes a deep breath. "There are a few more things in the report, but I can stop now if you want."

"No," I say. "Tell us everything."

What do I care? What's another bit of horrible news to add to my growing pile? My life is already a heap of shit—I might as well know what I'm dealing with.

Gabe's face crumples, and he nods.

Charlie takes a deep breath. "Well, obviously all we had were skeletal remains, so we weren't able to test any of the soft tissue."

I cringe and try to forget who he's talking about.

"Looks like she ingested the arsenic," Charlie continues. His voice is strained. "We were able to trace the purchase of the poison to Father's old advisor, Talin Thorne. We're not sure how he administered it, but we have enough evidence to prosecute."

I don't hear anything else he says. I already know what happened that day. I remember my father nodding to the pot of tea, saying that my mother would appreciate it. The dark look in his eyes, and the sick feeling in my stomach.

My sense of duty, and the love I had for my mother. I brought her the drink, feeling my father's eyes on my back. My mother kissed me on the forehead, and told me what a sweet boy I was.

She'd been reading a book, and she'd finished the whole pot.

I went to bed in my room, and when I woke up, she was dead.

It was me. I killed her.

Noise is screaming in my ears. My head is pounding, and my throat is dry. I can't speak. I try to focus on Charlie's lips— he's saying something, but I can't hear it.

I suck a breath in through my nose and push myself up to my feet. I don't know how I make it to my bed chambers, but somehow, I do.

The rest is a blur. I hyperventilate, standing in the middle of my room as it spins around me. I grab a pillow and scream into it. I punch the wall.

I hate myself.

Crumpling onto the floor, I start laughing. I thought medical school was my calling? I thought it was a way to make up for my mother's death? A way to make sure that I could stop that from happening to someone else?

How fucking naive could I be? How fucking stupid am I?

Medical school isn't my calling—it's my atonement. I always knew the truth, deep down in the bottom of my heart. That's why I am the way I am. That's why I need pain. That's why I know I'm not fit to be a king, or a prince, or part of this family at all.

Medical school was my penance. Giving up my royal privilege was my punishment.

Now, I know why.

I lay on the thick rug that covers my floor and I laugh. Someone pounds on the door, but the lock holds. I just laugh, and laugh, and laugh.

I choke on my laughter. Turning on my side, I cough and splutter, and then I take a painful breath. My ribs hurt, as if a giant's hand is squeezing my bones, crushing me with the weight of my own guilt.

On my hands and knees, I take a breath and heave myself onto my feet.

I never deserved Dahlia, and I certainly don't deserve to be the father of her child. She's better off in a coma than she is with me.

Self-pity is ugly, but it's addictive.

I shouldn't be a doctor. I shouldn't be a prince. I shouldn't be anything. What a fool I was, to think I deserved Dahlia's love! I thought that she completed me, that I had a right to the happiness she delivered!

All I gave her was a baby she never wanted, and a bee sting that might kill her.

I shouldn't be in this castle. I shouldn't be anywhere near the people that I love. I'm no good for anyone. All I bring is pain.

But I'm weak, and I know I need to see Dahlia again. I need to touch her skin one last time before I go away. I need to tell her the thing that I was too scared to utter while she was awake.

I need to tell Dahlia that I love her.

And that's what I do. I make my way to the hospital, my hands gripping my car's steering wheel so hard my fingers go numb. Every breath makes pins and needles pierce my lungs. I stumble to her floor and glance through the window to her room.

By some slight grace, she's alone.

I slip inside the room and sit on the chair by her bed. She doesn't stir. She doesn't move. Intertwining her fingers into mine, I let the tears drop from my eyes.

My heart is rotten—it has been since I was a child. It died long ago, along with my mother.

With Dahlia, I thought I had a chance at a better life—but I was wrong. The only thing I did was bring my misery onto her.

She thought she was cursed? The only curse she had was the one that brought me into her life.

Tears drop from my face onto her arm, and I wipe them off gently.

"I love you, Dahlia," I whisper. "If there was any way for my heart to love someone, you showed me how. I love you, and I love the child you're carrying."

My breath catches, and I cup her cheek. "I love you, and I'm so sorry."

Leaning over her, I press my lips to hers one final time. My tears wet her cheeks, and I brush them away, feeling the softness of her skin once more.

Hope flutters in my heart as her eyes move under her eyelids. My breath stills and I stare at her... but nothing happens.

She doesn't wake up, and I know there's no hope for me.

# 33

# DAHLIA

*They tease me now, telling me it was only a dream. But does it matter whether it was a dream or reality, if the dream made known to me the truth?*

—Fyodor Dostoyevsky, The Dream of a Ridiculous Man

# DAHLIA

## 34

# DAMON

I GLANCE at the clock as I leave Dahlia's room. She's been in a coma for ninety-six hours.

For four days, she's been lying in that hospital bed. For four days, I've prayed for her to wake up. I've suffered, and ached, and hoped, and died in every moment since I learned she was here.

I don't have the heart to look at her again, so I just walk out of her hospital room and leave. I exit the hospital, and I know I won't be coming back. I get in my car and drive to Grimdale.

There's no resisting now—no stopping me from doing what I've been wanting to do since this nightmare started. I drive to the warehouse as the sun disappears over the horizon. I don't bother locking the car—who knows if I'll come out of here again?

When I walk inside, the first fight is happening. I see Nigel approach me out of the corner of my eye.

"Your Highness," he says with a nod. "We haven't seen you in a while. The royal treatment?" His lips tug into a small grin.

I shake my head. "I'm going in the ring."

Nigel's eyes widen. "But, sir..."

I pinch my lips and turn my head to the fight happening in the ring. One of the men has his opponent against the ropes, pummeling his ribs mercilessly. The other man's head lolls from side to side.

The first man takes a step back and hits the other with a punishing uppercut. Blood splatters out of the other man's mouth, and shards of teeth go flying.

He collapses into a heap as victor raises his arms in triumph. The bloodthirsty screams of the onlookers ring in my ears. They cheer as the losing man is dragged away.

This is where I belong.

I belong in a den of pain and depravity. My true self is a bloody and battered savage. My heart is black, and my soul is dead.

I step into the ring before Nigel can stop me, and a hush falls over the spectators for a fraction of an instant. They all recognize me.

Then, the shouting begins. Their faces snarl at me from the other side of the ropes, and I stare at them blankly. I don't even care who my opponent is. I don't care who they are.

All I care about is suffering.

And suffer, I do.

Ravi steps into the ring amidst cheers and screams. I face him, letting my arms hang loose at my sides. For the first time in my history at this warehouse, I'm going to fight back.

The first punch hits me in the gut and I double over in pain. Ravi hits me again in the ribs, and the agony explodes through my chest.

I groan, straightening myself up. I can hear the shouts of the crowd, and the pounding of my blood in my ears. I can smell the sweat dripping from everyone's skin, and the dampness of the warehouse.

Ravi turns toward me, his nostrils flaring slightly as he stares me down.

He swings a meaty hand at me again, but I duck under it, landing a blow to his kidney. He shouts, more surprised than hurt. His neck reddens, and his eyes flash with anger.

I laugh.

His fist connects with my jaw. I go flying against the ropes, collapsing to my knees as I spit blood and chunks of teeth out. Ravi stands over me, waiting for me to stand up.

He knows this isn't over.

On wobbly feet, I stand before him. Every breath hurts. Ravi grunts and lumbers toward me.

My fist connects with his ribs, then his jaw, and then he roars and flings me over to the other side of the ring. The crowd is wild around us. Photos are prohibited here, but I see a flash.

It doesn't matter.

Ravi swings at me again. I duck, but not quite fast enough. He clips the edge of my head, sending pain shooting through my temple.

What is pain, though, when I know that I killed my own mother? What is agony, when Dahlia might die because of me? She'd never have been in my aunt's crosshairs had I not been seeing her. She probably wouldn't have been at the castle at all.

The big man's punches are nothing compared to the suffering I feel inside. He hits me again, and again, and again. My arms hang limply and I trip over my own feet.

I know I've lost. Blood pours out of my mouth, and my ears won't stop ringing.

It doesn't matter, though. Why would it?

I gather my strength for one last assault. Launching myself at my opponent, I somehow dodge his first punch and land a blow to his gut. He grunts and I have a split second to punch him again.

I'm not a trained fighter—that's Charlie's thing.

But I have instinct. I have pain.

I have nothing to lose.

With one strong uppercut from my left hand, Ravi stumbles backward. His eyes look dazed—and I laugh. I laugh because I might actually win this fight. I laugh because in my whole miserable life, I've never been good for anything.

Maybe this is my calling—beating another man in a dirty warehouse, while onlookers place bets on how many of my ribs he'll smash.

My victory is short-lived, though. A laugh is still on my lips when Ravi's eyes snap back to me. I don't even see the punch coming until his fist connects with the side of my head.

In the split second before I pass out, I hear a crunch. I feel the sweetest, most beautiful agony I've ever felt in my life, and I feel free.

I'll never be a doctor. I'll never atone for my sins. I'll never forgive myself for what I've done. This, right here—this brutal, savage beating—this is the true essence of my soul.

In that instant, I receive everything I've been looking for. Physical pain to match the suffering in my heart, punishment for my bad deeds, and finally, freedom from my own mind.

I fall into the darkness without another thought and without any hesitation. I welcome the abyss, and I hope I never wake up.

# DAMON

*Sad that our finest aspiration*
   *Our freshest dreams and meditations,*
   *In swift succession should decay,*
   *Like Autumn leaves that rot away.*

—Aleksandr Pushkin

# DAHLIA

I OPEN MY EYES. I'm alone.

You'd think that I would panic in this situation—that I might worry about why I'm lying in a hospital bed, with tubes sticking out of my arms and machines clicking by my bedside.

I don't panic, though.

Taking a deep breath, I feel completely at peace.

Damon loves me. He knows about the baby, and he loves it, too. I let my hand slide over my stomach as a smile stretches my lips.

It takes great effort to move my arm. My body feels weak —so, so weak. I try to adjust myself on the bed, groaning at the effort.

My mother and three aunts come crashing through the door.

"Dahlia!" Theresa exclaims. "You're awake!"

My mother falls on top of me, covering me in kisses. I do my best to lie there and breathe, until my aunts pull her off me. Her cheeks are wet and her eyes are shining.

"I thought we'd lost you," she sighs.

"Well, if you smother her like that, we might lose her again," Aunt Helen chides.

"Oh, stop." Aunt Margie smiles at me. "Good to see you, kid."

"You too." My voice is raspy. I smile with great effort. It's like my muscles are just remembering how to move again. "How long... What..." I inhale with difficulty. I can't even think of the right words. It feels like my mind has been scooped out of my head, and there's nothing left in my skull.

Theresa takes my hand and squeezes it. "It's been..." She glances at the clock. "One hundred hours, almost exactly."

"That's..." I frown. Math is hard. "Four days?"

"Just over," Margie says. "Four days and four hours—and don't we know it. Worst four days and four hours of my life." She's got her hands on my feet, massaging them gently. My mother has my other hand in hers, and Helen is stroking my calf.

"I feel like I've been hit by a bus," I groan.

"You had an anaphylactic reaction to a bee sting," Theresa explains. "I didn't even know there were bees out in the winter."

"Honeybees don't hibernate," I say, and then frown. How do I know that? I don't remember being stung by a bee.

"I blame that Malerie—that *witch*," my mother spits. Her cheeks turn bright red and she shakes her head. "It's her fault. She did this. She could have killed you!"

"Shh, Tabitha," Margie says. "Dahlia has just woken up. Don't upset her."

"I'm fine," I croak. I don't sound fine, or feel fine, but I say it anyway. My mother trembles in her seat, squeezing my hand and stroking my face.

I take a deep breath and reach back into my mind to try to remember what happened. My last memory is of calling

Damon from the lab and telling him I would be baby Charlie's godmother. I frown, trying to remember anything else.

It's a complete blank.

"Where's Damon?"

My aunts and mother all exchange loaded looks. My chest squeezes, and the machine next to my bed starts beeping. A nurse appears in the doorway.

"Everyone out!" She motions to my aunts and mother. "Out, out, out!"

"I'm staying." My mother's lips sour.

"It's okay, Mom," I say, "really."

She hesitates, and I try to smile at her.

My mother sighs. "We'll be right outside."

I nod, and the four of them leave. I let out a deep breath, and the nurse smiles at me.

"Overwhelmed?"

"Very."

"Well, you're in Farcliff Royal Hospital. We've been monitoring you since you came in, and everything seems to be okay. We'd like to run some tests now that you're awake. The doctor will come and see you in a little bit. Does that make sense?"

I nod.

"Can you tell me your name?"

"Dahlia Raventhal."

"Good. Date of birth?"

I tell her. The nurse runs through a few basic questions and is satisfied when I remember them all.

"Do you remember the bee sting?"

I shake my head. "I don't remember anything that happened before this," I say, motioning to the bed. "I just remember being at college that day."

"Sometimes, during severe trauma, memories are lost."

"Will they come back?"

"Maybe," the nurse says. "Often, they do. Sometimes, fragments come back. Sometimes, the mind just erases the trauma completely. The doctor will be able to answer your questions. For now, I want you to rest. Can I get you anything?"

I shake my head. She leaves the room, closing the door behind her. I hear a bit of commotion outside the door, and I'm able to deduce that she won't let my mom and aunts back in.

A few minutes later, the nurse returns with some water and a little cup of apple juice. "We've been feeding you through that tube for the last four days," she explains. "Still, I thought you might like a drink."

"Thanks." I watch her wheel them to my bedside. She nods to me and starts walking away when I stop her.

"Can you tell Prince Damon that I'm okay?"

The nurse's eyebrow arches the slightest bit.

"Please," I beg.

She nods slightly and slips out through the door. I lay there for a moment, trying to make sense of it all. The baby's fine. I'm fine.

I need to talk to Damon.

Turning my head to the bedside table, my eyes land on the drinks she brought. I gulp them down so fast the liquid doesn't touch the sides of my mouth. The juice tastes like the sweetest nectar I've ever had and I drink it in mere seconds, and then I fall back into bed with a sigh.

My stomach hurts from drinking so fast, but I can't bring myself to be upset about it. I've never enjoyed water and juice as much as I enjoyed those.

Just as I'm wiping a few stray drops of water off my hospital gown, there's a knock on the door. A doctor comes in, and she runs through the same basic questions the nurse had. She explains what happened to me—from the bee sting, to the anaphylaxis, to the coma.

"Your tests so far have been clear, but we'd like to keep you for observation. Were you aware that you're pregnant?"

I nod.

"Okay. Who is your doctor?"

I inhale sharply and shake my head. "I don't have one."

"You're about two months on, Dahlia. You should be having regular doctor's visits."

"I know. It's... complicated."

The doctor nods and jots down a note. "The father?"

"Prince Damon of Farcliff," I answer, trying to keep my voice as steady as possible.

The doctor looks up sharply and stares at me for a moment. "You're sure about that?"

I nod. "Can I get my phone please? I'd like to call him."

"I'll see what I can do." She puts her pen in her front pocket and slips the chart down into the slot at the end of my bed. "Get some rest."

I nod, and she leaves. This time, my family is allowed to come back in. My father is here now, his face lined with worry. It looks like he hasn't slept in days. He throws his arms around me and sobs into my neck. My eyes prickle, and I comfort him as best as I can.

My three aunts and my parents stay with me until I fall asleep again, and they take shifts through the night as well. I'm never alone for a moment. When I wake up again in the morning, Theresa smiles at me.

"Hey, kid," she says with a smile. "You look better today. You've got some color."

"I feel better," I say, tilting the hospital bed up to a seated position. My aunt fusses with my pillow and when I'm comfortable, I take a deep breath. "Theresa, where's Damon?"

She shakes her head. "I'm not sure, dear. We went to the castle and got your phone," she says, motioning to the side table. "Try him."

My aunt gives me a moment of privacy, and I try calling him three or four times. It rings out every time.

For the first time since I woke up, real worry starts to twist in my stomach.

# 37

# DAHLIA

I THINK the nurse in my room almost passes out from shock when Queen Elle strides through the door. Elle throws her arms around me and holds me tight.

"Oh my gosh, Dahlia! You scared me."

"I'm fine," I smile. "Have you heard from Damon?"

"Is he..."

"...the father?"

Elle nods.

"Yeah," I chuckle. "Like two peas in a pod, you and I."

"I remember a time that you were *very* high and mighty about using protection," she grins. "Look at you now—just as pregnant as I was."

I laugh, and my face feels like it's creaking from the effort. Elle plonks herself down in a chair and looks around the room. "I'm glad you're awake." When she looks at me again, her eyes are shining with tears. "I was scared."

"I'm sorry."

"Don't be," she says, waving a hand. "What do you have to be sorry for?"

"I don't know. Not telling you about me and Damon?"

Elle grunts, nodding. "Why didn't you?"

"I was scared."

The Queen chuckles and shakes her head. "What do you have to be scared of, Dahlia? You basically helped me survive through my last year at college. I'm happy that you and Damon are together—it means we'll always be close."

"It's not like we're married," I smile sadly. "He's not answering his phone."

The door to my room flies open and the two of us jump. It's Elle's security detail chief. He bows.

"Your Majesty, it's the King's brother, Damon."

"What about him?" I sit up. My heart starts thumping and the machine next to my bed starts beeping. Elle puts her hand on my arm to comfort me.

"He's downstairs, in the emergency department, ma'am." The agent looks from me, to Elle, and back to me again.

"I'm coming." I push myself up and promptly collapse back onto my bed.

"Stay there, Dahlia," Elle insists. "I'll find out what's going on."

I try to lift myself up again, but Elle puts her hand on my shoulder—not that I could move, anyway. My head is already spinning just from trying to sit up. There's no hope that I'd be able to use my legs right now, or be upright for any length of time.

Damon is hurt, though, and I need to know what's going on.

This is my fault. I should never have pushed him away. I shouldn't have hidden the baby from him. I should have faced my fears and been honest with him from the start.

Elle squeezes my shoulder. "I'll be back in a bit, okay? Stay calm."

Easier said than done. Elle strides from my room and I'm

left alone again. I lie back in bed, breathing raggedly. Staring at the ceiling, tears prickle my eyes.

There's only one thing I know for sure, now—that I love Prince Damon. I've loved him for weeks. Months, even. I've been carrying his child, and I've been too chicken to tell him about it.

My cowardice makes my cheeks burn with shame. I feel like a fraud. I pretend to be a carefree, happy girl, but I don't have the courage to live my life as honestly as I should.

I don't even have the courage to tell the man I love how I feel.

And now? What if I never get the chance?

My father pokes his head through the door. He smiles sadly at me and sits at the side of my bed. "I sent your mother and your aunts back to the castle," he says. "Didn't want you to be too crowded."

He threads his fingers into mine and I nod. "Thanks, Dad."

"You love Prince Damon?"

I sigh. "Yes."

My father nods. "Good."

"What's going on? Is he going to be okay?"

"I don't know, kiddo. I hope so." He squeezes my hand and takes a deep breath. "He was found at the entrance to the hospital. He was dropped off by someone, probably. We don't know who. He looks like he's been beaten badly."

My heart breaks. My lip trembles and I try to contain my tears. I know where he was, and I know what he did.

He asked for that beating.

My father wipes a tear from my cheek. "He stayed at the hospital almost the whole time you've been here. Your mother wouldn't let him in the room."

My father glances at me and shakes his head, his lips tugging in a slight smile.

"Maybe it's because I'm a man," he continues, "but I felt sorry for him. I could see what he was going through. He loves you too."

"I know." I say the words quietly as I close my eyes.

Of course Prince Damon loves me. He stayed at my house in Grimdale for weeks to be with me, instead of staying at the castle. He agreed to keep our relationship private because it's what I wanted. He made me feel like I was the only woman in the world.

Then, he watched me lay in this hospital bed, wondering if I'd ever wake up.

It feels like a weight is crushing my chest, and I can't take a full breath. Now Damon's somewhere in this hospital, too, and I'm the one worrying that he won't wake up.

I open my eyes again and glance at my father.

"Dad?"

"Yeah, kid?"

"I want to be there when he wakes up."

My father smiles at me. His eyes shine as he leans over to kiss my forehead.

"Okay," he says, nodding. "I'll see what I can do."

Exhaustion grips me again, and I fall into a fitful sleep. I dream in vivid detail of horrible, violent scenes. I wake up every few minutes, covered in a thin sheen of sweat. My father is always there, mopping my brow as I drift off again to a land of nightmares.

When I wake up, I'm not sure reality is any better.

# 38

# LADY MALERIE

MALERIE'S MOUTH goes dry as she races toward the Farcliff Royal Hospital. Her hands shake, and her steps are hurried. She pushes the door open with so much force it slams into the wall behind it. Heads turn toward her and nurses make outraged noises in response.

Malerie doesn't care.

"Damon Farcliff," she snaps. "Where is he?"

A nurse leads her toward her nephew's room. The nurse walks so damned slow. Too slow! Does no one hurry in this hospital? Don't they understand who she is—who Damon is?

"He's out of surgery now, and he's stable," the nurse explains as they near his room. "He's still asleep and probably will be for a while."

Malerie hardly hears her. She pushes the door open and a strangled scream escapes her lips.

Her nephew. Her boy. Her sweet, sweet Damon.

He's almost unrecognizable. His face has been battered, and his body is covered in bandages. A tube is sticking out of his side and a brace is around his neck.

Malerie falls against his bed, gasping.

This wasn't supposed to happen. None of this was supposed to happen.

"He was fighting at an illegal fight club," Queen Elle says from the doorway behind Malerie.

Malerie spins around. As she composes herself, she inclines her head toward the monarch. "A fight club?"

"Videos and pictures are already surfacing online." The Queen takes a few steps toward the bed, and Malerie has to hold herself back from lunging protectively in front of Damon. Her hands tremble, and she grips the side of the bed as hard as she can.

"Charlie told me he found out about his mother's poisoning and disappeared. A few hours later, he was dumped outside the emergency department." The Queen shakes her head, staring at Damon. "He's been a mess ever since he found out about Dahlia and the baby."

*The baby.*

So, it's true.

Malerie saw the way Dahlia had clutched her stomach—the way only a mother shields her unborn child.

In that moment, Malerie knew—but she hadn't believed it until now.

Malerie rakes in a deep breath and swings her eyes over to Damon. He's like a son to her, and seeing him on this hospital bed cuts Malerie to the bone. The pain in her chest is almost unbearable. She shakes her head.

He impregnated a *Raventhal*?

"How is Miss Raventhal doing?" Malerie manages to say. *Dead, I hope.*

She shouldn't think these things. Of course she shouldn't—but Malerie can't stop herself. Thoughts swirl around, and around, and around in her mind—until she feels like she's driving herself insane.

"Dahlia is awake now, thank goodness." The Queen responds.

"I'm glad." Malerie swings her eyes back to Damon.

She's not glad. The Raventhal girl is awake, and Damon is unconscious. This isn't the way it's supposed to be—but it's the way things always are with the Raventhals. They only bring death and destruction wherever they go.

Malerie turns back to the Queen, finally registering what Her Majesty said earlier.

"Poisoned?"

The Queen sighs, taking a seat next to Damon. "I thought Charlie told you. They found out she was poisoned with arsenic."

"Arsenic?" It's all Malerie can do to repeat the Queen's words. She stares at the monarch, and then at Damon. Her throat closes up, and it's hard to take a full breath. She swallows, wavering on her feet.

This was the Raventhals, she's sure of it. That *bitch*, Tabitha Raventhal, had her sights on the former Queen for years—and now, Dahlia got what she wanted too.

Malerie didn't intend for Dahlia to get stung by that bee. If she'd known what would happen, Malerie would have brought the entire hive inside. It would have been a good riddance.

The Raventhals have brought nothing but trouble down onto Farcliff. Malerie has never trusted any of them, but it's too late to do anything now. She glances at Damon, and hopes it's not too late for him, too.

A noise at the door makes Malerie turn her head. Young Dahlia is being wheeled in by her father.

Never in her life has Malerie felt rage like this. Dahlia is pale, hardly recovered from her anaphylaxis. She's gripping onto the sides of the wheelchair as if she's afraid she'll fall out of it. Her father wheels her in beside the Queen, and Malerie stares at the three of them with daggers in her eyes.

How *dare* they? How dare they walk into this room and pretend they care? How dare they come anywhere near Damon?

*They did this.*

They caused this. They killed the former Queen, and now they'll kill Damon, too.

"Get out," she spits.

Dahlia's eyebrows jump up. "What?"

"Get *out*. Both of you. You're not welcome here."

"They are welcome everywhere in Farcliff," the Queen warns.

Malerie bristles, pointing at Dahlia. "This is your fault. Your mother murdered the Queen, and now you're here to cause more havoc. Arrest them, Your Majesty! Don't be fooled by them. They're *murderers*."

She inhales sharply, trembling. She grips onto the end of the bed to hold herself back from lunging at the sick girl.

Dahlia stares at her, wide-eyed. "What?"

"Your mother killed the Queen, and you know it."

"She did not!" Dahlia's cheeks go pink and her father straightens up. The tension in the room heightens.

Malerie opens her mouth, ready to fling a string of insults at the two Raventhal vermin. They will *not* infest the castle again. She won't let it happen.

Before she can say anything, a rasping voice comes from the bed.

"No," Damon croaks. "I killed her."

# 39

# DAMON

My whole body is one, thumping ache. I can't think straight, but Dahlia is beside me and she's awake.

*She's alive.*

Oh, I never thought I'd see her eyes again. I thought I'd die on that warehouse floor with nothing but my memories of her.

But she's here, staring at me with tears in her eyes. The first spark of joy goes off in my heart at the sight of her smile.

My aunt is fuming at the end of the bed, and it takes all my energy to tear my eyes off Dahlia and speak again.

"My father..." I take a breath, "...gave me tea to bring her that night." I breathe in again, and everything hurts. My left side is throbbing, and I glance down to see a tube sticking out of it. I grimace.

"Tea?" My aunt asks, frowning.

"Yeah."

What was I saying?

Dahlia reaches over, slipping her hand into mine. She has an IV pole beside her, and she looks deathly pale—but she's *alive.*

I try to smile, but everything hurts. I cough, and pain explodes through me.

It's not the good kind of pain. Not the pain that I've been craving. This is too much. I've gone too far. It's wrong.

Dahlia lets out a long breath. "You're alive."

"So are you," I smile, and my face aches again.

"Damon," Aunt Malerie says, "are you suggesting you think my brother poisoned his own wife?"

"All the evidence points to it," I say and then take another labored breath. "We just didn't know how. Now we know. Poison—and I'm the one who gave it to her. Talin Thorne procured it, brought it to the castle, Father made the tea... and I delivered it to her."

Everyone stares at me, and I don't know what else to say. I don't even know what I feel. Shame still coats the inside of my mouth, but the look on Dahlia's face makes me think that everything will be okay. She leans over to kiss my hand, and rests her forehead against my arm.

I sigh.

My aunt is still trembling at the foot of my bed. I look at her, and she stares between me and Dahlia with fury in her eyes.

I don't understand it. I don't get what she's looking for in Dahlia—or why she thinks Dahlia's had anything to do with the Queen's death.

Aunt Malerie shakes her head. "It can't be."

"It was me," I say, closing my eyes to compose myself.

"No, Damon," my aunt whispers. "It couldn't be. You wouldn't do that."

"I did it, and I'll never forgive myself. I didn't know what I was doing, but I did it." I look away from them all, staring at the wall. My whole body is in pain, but it's not enough to get rid of the sick feeling in my stomach. It's not enough to wash me of the guilt and shame inside me. It hasn't taken away my past.

But then, Dahlia kisses my hand again, and sighs against me. Her breath is like a cool breeze washing over my skin.

Hope flames to life inside me.

If she's here, maybe there's a chance for my redemption? Maybe it's a sign that we're meant to be together. I look at her, ignoring the throbbing pain that's overtaking my entire body.

"The baby?" I whisper.

She glances up at me and a small smile appears on her lips. "It's okay."

"Good."

"You..." She inhales sharply and tears appear in her eyes. "Do you want it?"

"Of course I fucking want it," I say, laughing. The laugh makes pain shoot through my chest and I cough, and then groan.

Aunt Malerie still looks furious. She turns toward the door and gasps when Tabitha Raventhal darkens the doorway.

"What are you doing here?" Mrs. Raventhal spits at Aunt Malerie.

"I was going to ask you the same thing," my aunt replies. Her voice is spiked with venom.

Mrs. Raventhal's brow creases as she stares at Malerie, then to Dahlia, to me, and finally to her husband.

She curtsies for the Queen, but otherwise stays completely still.

"Are you happy now?" Malerie hisses, taking a step toward Mrs. Raventhal. "Are you happy with the destruction your family has caused?"

"Malerie," I start. My aunt ignores me.

"You came here fifteen years ago, and you killed the only

woman who was good for this Kingdom—and you had the nerve, the *audacity*, to blame my brother."

Tabitha's eyebrows arch, and then an ugly snarl twists her lips. "I never—"

"Stop," I say, and then cough at the pain of speaking. "Enough."

"Damon, they're blinding you. You think Dahlia loves you, but she doesn't. She's just trying to ensnare you, like her mother did to the Queen."

"Lady Malerie, that's *enough*," Elle snaps, her voice commanding and regal. "Your old feuds have no bearing here. The evidence doesn't point to the Raventhals."

Tension fills the air, and Malerie finally huffs and leaves the room.

Then, it's Tabitha Raventhal's turn to face us.

Exhaustion is settling into my bones. I can't take much more of this. I already know how Mrs. Raventhal feels about me, and right now, I don't care. I just want Dahlia to be beside me—safe, alive, and well.

"Dahlia, it's time to go back to your own room," Mrs. Raventhal says. She throws me a dirty stare and turns her nose up at me. "You shouldn't be here with *him*."

Dahlia squeezes my hand and straightens up in her wheelchair. Her chin juts out defiantly, and my love for her spreads through my chest.

"No."

"Excuse me?" Mrs. Raventhal says, arching an eyebrow.

"I said no. When I was a kid, you could ship me off to the mountains. I didn't have a say. You could fill my head with ideas that I was cursed, and that my life was doomed. But I'm not a kid anymore. This is the man I love, Mother." Her cheeks are bright red, and her shoulders are thrown back. "I love Damon Farcliff."

She glances at me and her eyes shine.

Turning back to her mother, Dahlia takes a deep breath.

"He's the man I want to marry, and he's the father of my child. I'm not leaving him just because you don't like his aunt. You and Malerie need to get over yourselves. Your stupid feud is hurting more people than just you two."

Mrs. Raventhal's mouth drops open. "I don't—"

"I don't care what you have to say," Dahlia interrupts. "You don't get to dictate what I do."

"I'm your mother."

"Congratulations. I'm going to be a mother, too, and I'll get to decide what's best for my baby—not you. Being with the baby's father is better than being shipped off to the middle of nowhere and being told that you're broken."

"Dahlia..." Her father tries to interject, but Dahlia puts her hand up.

"I understand your reasons for doing it, and I have no anger toward you—but it's time for me to be my own person. That means being with the man I love. If you want to be part of my life—and part of my baby's life—then you're going to have to deal with it."

Mr. Raventhal sighs. "I'll get the nurse to bring another bed in here."

"Harry, you can't let her stay!" Mrs. Raventhal exclaims, turning her anger to her husband.

"I can and I will," he retorts, before his voice softens. "Darling, she's right. This anger is only hurting us and the people we love. Let her be happy."

Mrs. Raventhal's lip trembles. Finally, she nods weakly.

Dahlia's father leads his wife out of the room, throwing the two of us one more glance. He gives his daughter a soft smile.

"I'm not leaving," Dahlia says to her father, even though

he never asked her to. Her mouth is set in a resolute line. A smile tugs at my lips. I love this girl more than anything in the world.

Her father sighs and turns his eyes to me. "You sure you can deal with her? Take it from someone who's spent the past thirty years with her mother—it's not going to change."

I grin. "I will gladly deal with her for thirty years and more."

Dahlia lays her head on my arm again. We stay there together, unmoving. It takes a few minutes for them to set up another bed and get Dahlia into it, but when they do, she's close enough to touch. She reaches her hand over to my bed and intertwines her fingers in mine.

Nurses check on us and family members fuss over us. When they finally leave, I turn to look at Dahlia.

"I thought you were gone."

"Is that why you went back to the warehouse?"

"You don't want to be with me, Dahlia," I say weakly. "Ever since I was a kid, I've just been hurting the people around me."

"You haven't hurt me."

"I did. I brought you to the castle and look at what happened."

"You didn't bring me anywhere. I went of my own free will." She smiles at me and shakes her head. "I don't even think your Aunt Malerie did it on purpose."

"I wouldn't put it past her."

"I don't know. I was watching her just now... She really cares about you. And so do I."

"You'll forgive her? Just like that?"

Dahlia takes a deep breath and stares at me for a moment, considering the question. Then, she nods. "Yeah."

"How? How do you forgive so easily?"

"Forgiveness is a choice." She smiles at me and squeezes my hand. "You have to give yourself permission to forgive and be forgiven."

I know she's talking about my mother. I know she's talking about me forgiving myself. She makes it sound so easy, but...

...what if it was?

What if I stopped fighting it, and I just let go of the pain? What if I let go of the darkness?

"You have to stop fighting," Dahlia says softly. "None of what has happened was your fault—not with your mother, or with me."

I grimace, turning my head to stare at the ceiling. "Yeah."

"I mean it."

I sigh. Her words start to sink in, but I wonder if I'll ever truly believe them.

But then, Dahlia squeezes my hand and a wave of calm washes over me.

"You have to forgive yourself, Damon. Otherwise you'll never find peace."

The only time in my life that I haven't been plagued by darkness has been when I'm with Dahlia. What if she's right? What if it is just as easy as deciding to accept forgiveness?

"I don't know how to forgive myself," I whisper.

Her hand is warm, and it fits perfectly into mine. She lets out a long breath. "You just decide to do it one day. You hold on to anger and pain until it feels like it's part of you, and then at one point you just... let it go."

Dahlia turns her head toward me and sighs. "I think the curse was my way of holding onto my anger and pain. I know, now, that being shipped off to the Rockies messed me up a little. Not knowing who I am..." She sighs. "...I don't think my parents are bad people, but they made bad decisions. My whole life, I was worried about doing things that would upset my mother. Now I know that I need to live my life without being crippled by the thought of how she'll react. I need to do what's best for me, and this baby—and you."

She smiles at me. "You showed me that the curse doesn't exist. I make choices, and they shape my life—just like everyone else."

"So, just go ahead and let it go, huh? Just like that?"

"Just like that." Dahlia stares at me and a smile stretches across her lips.

"You don't have a Russian quote for me? Now seems like the perfect time."

Dahlia thinks for a moment, chewing her lip and staring at the wall behind me.

"*Your worst sin is that you have destroyed and betrayed yourself for nothing.*" She glances at me. "Don't let it be for nothing, Damon."

"I thought you were going to say something about the power of love and forgiveness."

"It's Dostoyevsky, not Dr. Phil," she laughs.

She's too far away to kiss, and I'm in too much pain to move. But I squeeze her hand and smile at her. "Marry me, Dahlia."

Her eyebrows arch. "Really?"

"Really. I don't want to be apart from you ever again. I want you to be mine forever—and I want to be yours forever, too. You make me a better person. I want to do the same for you."

Her smile is so dazzling that it makes my heart thump in my chest. Her eyes sparkle with unshed tears. She nods. "Okay."

If I wasn't confined to a hospital bed, I'd shout out and

celebrate, and spin her around the room. As it stands, though, all I can do is smile and squeeze her hand.

"I love you," I whisper.

"I love you too." The two of us fall asleep beside each other—exactly where we were always supposed to be.

# EPILOGUE
## DAHLIA

DAMON and I spend another week in the hospital together. On the third day, a knock comes on the door. Lady Malerie sticks her head in, and Damon nods for her to enter.

Her face looks pinched, and more lines have appeared around her eyes. She sits down in a chair beside Damon's bed and takes a deep breath.

"I spoke to my brother," she says.

"And?" Damon asks.

Lady Malerie shakes her head. "Oh, Damon, I'm so sorry. I had no idea." Her eyes fill with tears and my chest squeezes. "He told me everything. He admitted everything. I'm so sorry." A tear rolls down her cheek. I've never seen her look so... *human.*

Lady Malerie swings her gaze to me and inclines her head. "Miss Raventhal, I know that forgiveness is a lot to ask, so I won't ask it of you. I was blind to my brother's crimes. He was King and I... Well, I guess I didn't want to believe that he was a bad person."

"We were all blind to it," I respond.

"Your mother wasn't."

"No," I admit.

Lady Malerie takes a deep breath. "I'm sorry—and I want you both to know that... Well, I'm happy for you—truly. I see the way you look at each other, and I hope that one day I'll find someone who loves me the way you love each other. I'll never forgive myself for the pain I've caused you and your family."

"Must run in the family," I grin.

"Excuse me?" Lady Malerie frowns.

Damon chuckles. "I think what Dahlia is saying is: she forgives you."

"Wholeheartedly," I respond. "I know you didn't mean to bring the bee inside, and I know that you were only trying to protect your family from what you saw as a threat." I pause. "But, Lady Malerie, can I ask you something?"

"Of course."

"Will you please try to talk to my mother? I'm not expecting you to be best friends, or anything—but I'd like it if you were civil." I glance at Damon, and we both smile. "I think I might be sticking around the castle for a while, which means you and my mom might be seeing each other quite regularly."

Malerie straightens her shoulders and nods. "I'll do my best."

I extend my hand toward her, and she grasps it in hers. She leans over Damon and presses a kiss to his cheek, and then leaves us alone again.

Damon exhales deeply and I smile at him.

"I respect that of her," I say. "That took a lot of guts to come in here and apologize like that."

"She's not a bad person," he says. "Although she does smell very oniony."

I laugh, nodding. "She does. That's actually fairly common with women."

"It is?"

"Uh huh," I nod. "Women excrete more sulfur when they sweat. It mixes with the bacteria that causes body odor—staphylococcus hominis—and makes an onion smell. Men excrete more fatty acids, so they smell like cheese."

Damon grins. "Let me guess—Chekhov said that?"

I nudge him, laughing. "Entry-level microbiology, Damon."

He just laughs, winking.

"I don't mind your aunt. I don't think she's a bad person, even if she does smell oniony."

"When I think about it now, she was around a lot after my mother died. I didn't think much of it then, but now... Maybe she does really care about my brothers and me."

I climb out of my bed and crawl in beside Damon in his. I'm a lot more mobile than he is—battered and bruised after his fight. He winces as I touch his chest, and I move my arm away. I settle in beside him, barely touching him but resting my head on his pillow. He leans his head against mine and lets out a sigh.

"I love you, Dahlia Raventhal..."

"...and I love you, Damon Farcliff. You know something?"

"What's that?"

"Us being together is a big deal—not just for our families, but for the Kingdom, too."

"How do you figure?"

"Well, it's like a new era. Your father was power-hungry, and cruel, and now Charlie is ushering in change. So are you. Forgiving my family and dating me is like a new beginning for Farcliff."

"What can I say? I live in service of the Kingdom." Damon grins, and then presses his lips to my temple.

WE DON'T LEAVE each other's side until we leave the hospital. Even then, I go back to Farcliff Castle with Damon and move into his chambers with him. The hundred hours I spent in a coma feel like they were a hundred years, and I never want to be apart from him again.

Damon makes me feel complete. Being with him shines a light into all the dark corners of my mind, where fears about my curse and doubts of my own abilities still lurk. He banishes them all, and gives me the strength to take on the world.

He gets his teeth fixed, and smiles more than ever before. Some of the scars on Damon's body won't ever disappear, but they remind us that things haven't always been this good.

It takes weeks before we both feel back to normal. The Farcliff tabloids publish story, after story, after story about us —until I feel like I'll never be accepted in Farcliff because I'm a Raventhal. Videos and photos of Damon's fight also go viral, and the press is especially vicious toward him.

We try to stay out of it, but it's hard to ignore every single news story. It's not until Malerie comes out in support of our relationship that the news stories start to change. Lady Malerie spends more time in Farcliff in the weeks when we recover, and I come to appreciate her presence more deeply than I could have thought.

She's not a warm woman, but she's strong. I appreciate her unwavering sense of self, especially when I've struggled to find my own way in the world. I also appreciate the effort she makes in reconciling with my mother. The two women find an uneasy sort of civility with each other, and I decide that's enough for now.

Baby Charlie's christening is beautiful, and at the end of it, Lady Malerie wraps me in a big, onion-smelling hug afterward. Is it strange that I find her scent almost comforting now?

"I'm glad she chose you, Dahlia," Malerie tells me. "You'll be a wonderful godmother."

I FINISH my last semester at Farcliff University a few months ahead of my due date. Damon, on the other hand, decides not to finish medical school.

When I ask him about his decision, Damon sighs.

"I think I was doing it for all the wrong reasons. I thought it would make me a better person, or it would make up for what I'd done. After the fight..."

He takes a deep breath.

"...after everything came out in the press, I know that I'll never be able to be a normal person—not as a prince. They'll always tear me to shreds. I can't be a medical professional if I'm living under that kind of scrutiny."

"Shouldn't have chosen a Raventhal as a girlfriend, I guess."

"I didn't have a choice," he grins. "I couldn't have stopped myself if I tried."

I lean my head against his shoulder and close my eyes, smiling. "So, what are you going to do now?"

Damon sighs. "Well, I was thinking that I wanted to do something good for Farcliff. What do you think about a foundation for mental health? Supporting youth who are struggling. I could have used something like that, growing up."

I press a kiss to his cheek and smile at him. "I think that's a wonderful idea."

Life didn't turn out how I expect it to.

I came to Farcliff wanting to find out the truth about my past and about my family. I found it, and it's not a neat little story that I can lock away in my heart. The past is messy, and jagged, and full of hurt feelings and rancor that might never heal.

But by coming here, I also found love—and the love I have with Damon is worth any messiness that comes with it.

Our baby girl, Dawn, is born surrounded by happy tears and doting grandparents.

Damon and I get married six months later, in a similar ceremony to that of Elle and Charlie. It's just close friends and family—and no press, thank goodness.

At the wedding, I lean my head against Damon's shoulder, and watch our guests as they dance and drink. Near the edge of the room, my mother is rocking my baby girl and dancing along to the music. Malerie approaches, and I watch the two women smile over the child. My mother hands off my daughter to Lady Malerie, smiling, and my heart grows.

"They look like they're getting along," Damon says, following my gaze.

"Never thought I'd see the day."

"You brought us back together, Dahlia," Damon says, putting his arm around me.

I settle into his arms and let happiness wash over me. In his arms, I know that we've found the type of love that I didn't think existed.

We've found true love. A love that runs deep and strong. A love that doesn't waver and doesn't hesitate—the kind of love that lasts until the end of time.

# EXTENDED EPILOGUE

# DAHLIA



"ARE YOU SURE YOU'RE OKAY?" Damon's eyebrows draw together.

I nod. "I want to learn."

Brushing the dust off my shorts, I pick myself up off the floor and stand my bicycle up. A small drip of blood trails down from my scraped knee, and I ignore it. Now is not the time to let a little scuff stop me.

Yes, I'm nearly thirty years old, and no, I don't know how to ride a bike.

That's about to change.

I grip the handlebars and swing a leg over it.

Damon checks my helmet and gives me a nod, stepping back. "You can do it. I believe in you."

Taking a deep breath, I look at the stretch of deserted castle pathway in front of me.

A noise coming from Damon breaks my concentration. I glance over at him to see him wiping a smile off his face.

"What?"

"Nothing." He shakes his head.

"Tell me."

"You're cute, is all. You get this really serious expression on your face like you're about to go for a world record."

"Well, it might be a world record for someone as old as me to be learning how to ride this thing."

Damon grins again, and quickly hides it. "Come on," he says. "Let's try again. Remember, the faster you go, the more stable you'll feel."

I take a deep breath and nod. "Okay."

My hands grip the handlebars and I stare down the path. This is ridiculous—I know it is. My two kids—toddlers—can almost ride their bikes better than I can. I'm a college graduate, I've been married for over five years, I have two children... but I can't pedal down a road without falling over.

Well, today is the day. I'm going to learn how to ride this bike if it's the last thing I do. With one foot on the pedal, I fill my lungs once more. I ignore the burning skin on my knee, and I stare down the pathway...

...and I push off.

Wobbling, I put my other foot on the pedals and start going. The bike shakes and I almost lose control, but then I remember Damon's words.

The faster I go, the easier it'll be.

I love him and I trust him, so I do as he says. I grind my teeth together and start pedaling like I've never done before. Around and around and around my feet go, and pretty soon I'm flying down the path. Damon's footsteps pound behind me.

"Keep going, Dahlia! You can do it!"

The wind rushes around my face as my adrenaline pumps. As I pick up speed, a smile stretches over my lips.

I'm doing it. I'm riding a bike! Finally, after years of avoiding it, years of being scared of it, *I'm doing it.* Nothing can stop me now!

Laughter bubbles up inside me as I go faster and faster. Damon calls out encouragement, still running behind me. I can hear his labored breaths behind me, but I don't care.

I'm flying. I'm going so fast I feel like I'm about to take off. I pedal and pedal, going faster down the pathway as more and more laughter comes out of me.

My grip on the handlebars loosen as euphoria floods my veins.

I've been afraid of this my whole life. I haven't wanted to learn, and as I got older, it became less and less of an issue. When Damon bought me this bike last year, I left it in the garage for months without touching it.

I was letting my fear stop me. I was letting this little bicycle control me.

Well, not anymore.

I can't keep the smile off my face. I pedal harder, picking more speed. The pathway inclines slightly downward, and pretty soon I'm travelling faster than I've ever done before. Damon's footsteps are fading in the distance, but I can still hear the words of encouragement he calls out to me.

And then, I wobble—and catch myself.

My heart thumps, and I grip the handlebars more tightly. My breath hitches, and sweat gathers between my shoulder blades. I've already fallen once today, I'm not going to do it again.

But the path is getting steeper, and I don't feel entirely equipped for this kind of speed. My front tire catches on a pebble, and I wobble once more.

Again, I catch myself and right the bike. By now, I can

taste blood in my mouth. My teeth are gnashing together as my heart leaps in my throat.

The pathway dives down steeper, and I start to scream. "Damon!"

"Brake!"

I can't think straight. How do I brake again?

*Wobble.*

"Brake, Dahlia!"

Words aren't working. How the heck do I brake on this thing? I pedal backwards, but that just makes me wobble some more.

"Damon!"

"Brake, Dahlia!"

"Try again!" His voice is fading in the distance, but I can't look back. All I can see is the hard asphalt of the pathway looming ahead of me. More scraped skin is in the cards for me, I can already tell. I'll be more bruised and battered than Damon was after the warehouse.

Fear spikes through me.

"I can't!"

*Wobble.*

Damon's footsteps are pounding on the pavement behind me. "Squeeze the handlebars! Or aim for the bushes!"

*Of course—the handlebars!*

At the bottom of the hill, a thick hedge looms. In the depths of my brain, I know what Damon said. He gave me two choices—brake, or aim for the bushes. But in the heat of the moment, my mind gets muddled. Somehow, I do both. I scream, turning the handlebars toward the bush and pressing down on the brake levers as hard as I can.

The bike stops, but I don't.

The crash isn't as bad as I expect. I go flying over the handlebars and land in the bush, which softens my landing considerably. The branches scrape up my arms and legs as I tumble through them, landing with an *oof* on the hard packed earth below.

Damon runs up to me, panting. He crouches down, pulling me from the bush and cradling me in his arms. "Are you okay?"

"I think so," I pant. I move my arms and legs. "I don't think anything's broken."

"Fucking hell, Dahlia."

"I forgot how to brake." I sit up, wincing as the stinging pain of a hundred scrapes and scratches starts to burn. I unclip my helmet and toss it to the side.

"Well, looks like you remembered," Damon says, standing up. He helps me to my feet and wraps me in a hug. "I'm sorry, Dahlia. Maybe we should stop there for today."

He pauses, and I can tell he's fighting back a smile. I don't even have to see his face to know he's on the verge of cracking up. He wraps his arms around me and a small chuckle slips through his lips.

"Damon..."

"I'm not laughing." A chuckle slips through his lips.

"It sounds like you're laughing."

"I'm not, I promise." He giggles "It's just the sight of you crashing into the bushes..."

I pull away from him, doing my best to look angry. The second I see his face, though, I know it won't last. The two of us break down into peals of laughter. Damon laughs loudly, with his mouth wide open. Every time he looks at me, he starts laughing again.

We quiet down, but then the Prince reaches over and pulls out a twig from my hair, and we start laughing again.

Finally, Damon pulls the bike out of the bush, leaving a

massive dent in the shrubbery. My bike looks no worse for wear, and we start heading back toward the castle.

I take a deep breath. "Well, at least I made it farther than last time."

"Well, you did pretty well. You picked up some speed!" Damon's eyes are gleaming, and I nudge him with my shoulder.

I try my best to keep my face serious. "I could have been hurt."

"Good thing there are lots of bushes around." He fights back a laugh, and I groan.

Damon is wheeling my bike and me carrying my helmet in one hand. My husband glances at me.

"You okay?"

"I'm just not sure I'm cut out to ride bikes."

"I don't get why it's so difficult for you."

"*Can a man who's warm understand one who's freezing?*"

Damon grins. "Tolstoy?"

"Solzhenitsyn."

"Ah, of course," he grins. "Well, things aren't too dire if you're still quoting the Russians."

"The Russians never had to learn how to ride a bike as an adult. Whoever said, 'it's just like riding a bike' had no idea what they were talking about."

My whole body aches, but every time I glance at Damon, all I want to do is laugh.

That's how the past five years have been. Every time I think something is difficult, every time I feel bad or angry or hurt, Damon makes me feel like everything will be okay.

So, when we round the last bend and make it to the castle, I have a smile on my face, too. Elle, the Queen, is there with two nannies, sitting on the grass with her youngest daughter in her arms. My two children are running around with her two eldest. She looks at us with wide eyes. As we get closer, her gaze drops to my scraped knees and scratched-up arms.

Her eyebrow arches. "How did the lesson go?"

"Dahlia did wonderfully," Damon grins.

Elle looks at my banged-up body. "Uh huh."

"Progress is progress," Damon says as another giggle escapes his lips. He reaches over and pulls another leaf out of my hair.

Elle fights to keep a grin off her face. Dawn, our eldest, runs up to me and wraps me in a big toddler hug. She leans over and kisses my knee.

"For your boo-boo."

"Thank you, Dawn," I say, leaning over to kiss her head. She runs off again with Little Charlie. The two of them have been inseparable since they were able to crawl.

One of the nannies produces a first aid kit, and Damon and I take a seat next to Elle. I tend to my scrapes and watch our children play. Damon drapes an arm over me and pulls me close.

"I'm proud of you," he whispers in my ear.

"For crashing into a bush?"

"For having the guts to try it, and for getting back up after you fall."

He lays a soft kiss on my lips, and I melt into his arms. King Charlie appears in the doorway with a basket full of food, and the four of us—with two nannies and five children —share some snacks and drinks on the castle lawn. Damon gives an excruciatingly accurate account of my dive into the bushes, and I laugh until my cheeks hurt.

"I would pay to see that," Elle grins, winking at me.

"I'd pay to have you *not* see it." I laugh, shaking my head.

"If Gabe were here, he'd be able to teach you in no time,"

Damon says. "He can do jumps and ticks on his bike—he was a bit of a daredevil when we were kids."

"Is he still at the country estate?"

Charlie grunts in response. His face darkens and he shakes his head. "Hasn't come back to Farcliff Castle in almost a year. I had to send one of our gardeners out there to make sure he was still alive."

Damon sighs, and the four of us fall silent. No one says anything until Dawn and Little Charlie come tumbling toward us. Their laughter brightens our moods, and I gather my daughter in my arms and cover her in kisses.

Elle and Charlie look as happy as I feel. Damon wraps his arms around us as our youngest, Damon Jr., comes flying into his embrace.

I may not be the best bike rider in the Kingdom, but I am the luckiest. Surrounded by friends and family, with happy, healthy children, I know that I'm the most fortunate woman in Farcliff. Damon puts his arm around me and kisses my temple.

"Same time tomorrow?"

"I might let these scrapes heal first." I lift up my battered arms and nod to my scuffed knees.

Damon chuckles. "Okay, deal. Next week, then."

"You're enjoying this far too much."

"I'd enjoy anything with you, Dahlia." He kisses me softly, and breaks away when a laugh tumbles out of him. "But yes, it was the best entertainment I've seen in weeks."

Before I can protest, he wraps me in his arms and lays a wet, loud kiss on my cheeks. I yelp and laugh, and our children jump on top of us and my heart overflows with gratitude.

I may not know how to ride a bike, but I do have a loving family and healthy, happy children. Elle smiles at me, winking. We stand up and head back to the castle—back to our home. I clean up my wounds and wrap my arms around my husband. I don't know if I'm deserving of this kind of happiness, but I am grateful for it.

"I love you, Dahlia," Damon says as he kisses the tip of my nose. I melt into his arms and sigh in contentment. Bruised and scraped as I may be, I've never felt better than I do right now.

～

LILIAN MONROE
CRUEL PRINCE
ROYALLY UNEXPECTED: BOOK THREE

# CRUEL PRINCE

ROYALLY UNEXPECTED: BOOK 3

1

———

**JO**

THE DOOR SLAMS, and my boyfriend of two years becomes my ex-boyfriend, as of right now.

I stand in the middle of my studio apartment, staring after Ryan. He's gone. I'm not even sure how I feel about it. Offended? Relieved? Indifferent?

Glancing over at my laptop screen, I flinch. A grimace lingers on my lips as I read the form letter for the fourth time. It's yet another rejection email from a publisher, and it stings. I'm more hurt about their rejection than Ryan's—and that's probably exactly why he left. Apparently, I care too much about my flagging writing career and not enough about his ego.

Should I care that he's gone? Does the fact that I don't make me a bad person?

I'm not heartless, I swear. Ryan was nice, I guess.

But he kept talking about marriage, babies, and me being a stay-at-home mom. Never once did he ask me if I really wanted that.

I stare at the door again, and then back at the email. I

scan my body, and decide that I do, indeed, care more about the publisher's rejection than I do about my ex.

My shoulders slump, and I sink down onto my desk chair.

Ryan and my relationship was probably over a long time ago, but I'd hung on in the vain hope that something would change. Our relationship was just like every other relationship that I've ever had—and like my short stint in college, or my current writing career: Another failure.

Just like this email. Rejection never gets easier—even if it's the thirtieth refusal letter I've received this month.

Reading the email over and over again, my heart sinks. Every publisher's snub is the same. It's professional, yet it cuts deep into the fabric of my once unshakeable confidence.

My manuscript didn't grip the editors, it says. The beginning wasn't compelling enough.

How much of my book did they read before rejecting it, I wonder?

I rub my hands over my face, sighing. That was the last publisher on my list. My book is dead. I'm single, broke, and apparently a big, old failure.

Look away while I wallow for a while, will you?

I push myself off my chair and stare around my apartment. My shifts at the restaurant aren't covering all my expenses. My freelance work has dried up, and I'm not sure how I'll make rent next month.

I came to New York City six years ago with big dreams and bigger expectations, and they haven't quite come to fruition. By 'haven't quite' I mean I should probably tattoo FLOP in big letters across my forehead. I've ended up with a big pile of rejection letters and a very small bank account.

Ryan was offering to help me out with my expenses until I got a book deal—but that's obviously not going to happen, now.

"That's fine," I say under my breath. "I didn't want your money anyway." I talk to the closed door, as if my ex-boyfriend can hear me.

Ryan used his money as a chain around my neck, always making me feel guilty for not having enough of my own. He'd make a big show of paying for things whenever I couldn't—which was often. I hated it.

But not anymore. I won't use him as a crutch. I'll figure this out on my own. I press my lips together and widen my stance. Pushing up my sleeves, I swing my eyes from one end of the room to the other.

Is my sofa worth anything? I don't even sit on it that much. Maybe I could get a hundred bucks for it. The TV can't be worth much—it's an old-style thing with knobs on the front and no remote—but maybe a hipster will want it in an ironic kind of way. My dining room table has three mismatched chairs and a lot of rings from coffee mugs on it. I doubt I'd be able to even give it away for free.

My eyes flick around the tiny studio apartment, cataloguing all my belongings. Only my two most precious possessions aren't for sale. My laptop and the little leather-bound notebook where I stuff all my ideas. Those two items will stay with me until I croak.

When my eyes land on my dresser, I pause. Maybe I could sell my dirty panties on the Internet, or something. Don't people pay a lot for those?

Shaking my head, I try to build myself back up again.

I'm not a screw-up. It's not failing until you stop picking yourself back up. Isn't that on a motivational poster somewhere?

Things will work out—they always do. I'll pick up a couple of extra shifts at the restaurant. I'll put my groceries on my credit card. I'll hustle harder for some freelance writing work. I'll sell my panties, if needs be.

I'll make it work. I can do it.

I stretch my neck from side to side and try to build myself back up. Maybe if I rewrite the book—revise it for the millionth time and make the beginning more gripping—maybe then a publisher will pick it up. I'll get a nice advance cheque, and my problems will be solved.

It'll happen. I have faith.

Confidence starts to creep into my heart. A sense of calm washes over me, and a smile drifts over my lips.

I haven't been rejected by my ex-boyfriend—I've been *freed*. I can do anything. I can *be* anything! I'm not Jolie, failed writer and tired waitress. Not anymore. No, I'm Jolie, the independent and successful boss-lady! Watch me blossom!

My smile grows wider as my belief in myself grows. I slam my laptop screen down with a thud as a giggle bubbles up inside me.

Laughter tastes sweet, even if I'm alone in my apartment. I throw my head back and let out a big belly laugh, leaning into the feeling.

*Freedom.*

It feels good. Great, even! I build myself higher, and higher, and higher...

...and then reality brings me crashing all the way back down when the lights in my apartment flicker off.

I hear the refrigerator shut down, too, as the power to my entire apartment is cut.

"Shit, shit, shit." I rush to the switch on the wall. I flick the lights on and off, but nothing happens. Using the flashlight on my phone, I find the electrical panel and turn the breakers on and off again, but nothing works. I try it again, and again, and again...

...nothing.

Groaning, I sink down to the floor. I drop my head in my hands and I admit to myself what I've known since the lights went off:

It's not the breaker. It's the bill.

To be precise, it's the red-marked bill currently sitting on my kitchen table, unopened and unpaid.

Tears sting my eyes as an overwhelming sense of failure creeps into my heart. How did I think I could do this? When I moved away from Farcliff, I truly believed I could make it in the world. I had eight hundred dollars, half of an English Lit college degree, and an ego the size of Farcliff Kingdom. I was invincible.

I got myself a work visa to the United States and I moved to New York, full of hope and dreams and naivety.

Bright-eyed, I fell in love with the lights and noise of the city.

Now, the lights are off and it's deathly quiet.

I've failed. Professionally, personally, and philosophically flopped.

My lower lip trembles as I squeeze my hands into fists. I dig my fingernails into my palms to try and get a grip on myself. I'm working the closing shift at the restaurant tonight, and the last thing I need to do is show up with puffy, blood-shot eyes and a red nose from crying.

I shut my eyes and try to pull myself together.

It feels like I'm teetering on the brink of a breakdown. A strong gust of wind would knock me into meltdown mode. I keep swinging between highs and lows every few minutes, and it's making my head spin. So, I just stay huddled on the floor, with my hands balled into fists and my eyes squeezed shut.

I count to a hundred. The lights still haven't miraculously come back on, and I'm still single and broke—but at least I don't feel like I'm going to break down and cry anymore.

Picking myself up off the floor, I stand up and find my work uniform. I'll work my shift tonight and scrape together enough money for the bill. The power will be back on in no time.

I repeat the words to myself over and over until I almost believe them. I take extra time to do my makeup and hair like I'm putting on war paint. I stare at myself in the mirror, fake-smiling at my reflection. I wonder if I look as miserable as I feel.

My phone rings, interrupting my pity-party. It's my mother.

"Hey, Mom."

"Jolie, don't panic."

You know when people say, 'don't panic' and you immediately start panicking? And then instead of explaining themselves, they pause, as if the silence hanging between you will do anything to calm your racing mind?

My mother is an expert at that. She wrote the book on dramatic pauses—which, coincidentally, is more than I can say about my own book-writing career.

"*Whatsgoingon?*" I breathe the words out as one.

"It's your father." My mother sighs.

My heart takes off at breakneck speed, trying its best to make me faint. "What happened?"

Is this the gust of wind that will knock me over the edge into a full-on breakdown?

"The cancer's back," she says quietly.

"No. No, no, no. How, Mom? How?"

"The oncologist said it's treatable, and we caught it very early this time. We're going to have to move back to Farcliff

City. We have to be near the hospital now. There aren't enough medical facilities out here in Westhill."

My parents have been living at the Westhill Palace, in the heart of the forests on the western edge of the Kingdom. My father has been in charge of the Westhill Royal Rose Gardens for about five years. The two of them moved to Westhill after I left for the United States. Being appointed to the Westhill Rose Garden was the greatest honor that has ever been bestowed upon my family.

For my parents to be moving away from the Westhill, it means my father's illness is getting very, very serious.

"What about the garden?" My voice squeaks, and I clear my tightening throat.

My mother sighs. "We're going to have to leave it behind. Harry Brooks will be in charge of it."

"Harry Brooks? Last time you left him in charge of the roses, you practically had to start over. He killed nearly all of them—you were complaining about it for months."

"Jolie..."

"Mom... How bad is it?"

Leaving Westhill on such short notice, *and* leaving the incompetent Brooks in charge of the Royal Rose Gardens means something is seriously wrong. My heart is racing and I'm finding it hard to see straight.

My mother sighs. "We just need to be closer to the hospital, that's all. He needs to start another course of chemotherapy, so we'll be in and out of the hospital every week. We can't travel two hours each way from Westhill to Farcliff. It's just not feasible."

"Every week?"

*Mental breakdown, here I come.*

"The doctors had to up the frequency of his treatment this time."

"I'm coming home."

"Jo, stop. You don't have to. Your father didn't even want me to tell you that we were moving, but I wanted you to know. Everything will be fine. He'll recover—we just need a bit more care for him this time. It's precautionary."

"Chemo isn't precautionary, Mom. *Aggressive* chemo isn't a precaution."

My mind is reeling. I can't stay here. I can't be in a foreign country, struggling to keep my lights on, when my father is in an out of the hospital.

"I'm coming home," I repeat.

"No, Jolie. You can't put your life on hold for us. You're doing so well in New York! It keeps your father and I going to know that you've been so successful."

I almost start laughing.

Successful? Me?

I'm the very definition of failure. I'm so far from success that I might as well not even know the meaning of the word. I've never told them how much I'm struggling, of course. What would that accomplish?

But the truth is, I wouldn't be giving anything up by coming home. I need to be close to my family. There's nothing left for me here.

Taking a deep breath, I try to think of an angle that my parents will agree to. "Well, what if I tended the rose gardens?" The words slip out of my mouth before I even know what I'm saying.

My mother pauses, and the words hang between us. "What do you mean?"

"I mean, I'm better at gardening that Harry fucking Brooks—"

"*Language*, Jolie."

"Sorry. All I'm saying is, I'll be closer to you. At least I'll be in the Kingdom. That way, Dad won't have to worry about the gardens going to shit—sorry, I mean he'll know the gardens are being taken care of. I can write from there, too. A bit of solitude in the country will do me good. I've been wanting to get away from the city, anyway."

I can hear my mother breathing on the other side of the line. She's thinking about it.

"Darling, the Prince..."

"I can handle the Prince."

"He's not well. Ever since he had his daughter..."

"Who cares? I probably won't even see him. You've lived in the Westhill for years, and you've only seen him a handful of times."

"Jo..."

"Mom, I want to be closer. If you won't let me stay with you in Farcliff, at least let me help out with the gardens. Dad will want to show some flowers at the Annual Rose Festival, no? How would he feel if he wasn't able to show any flowers at all?"

Mom sighs, and I can hear her starting to give in. "I'll talk to your father."

The tightness in my chest eases, and I nod. "Okay. I'll start packing."

I've always been decisive, but this is quick—even for me. The power isn't coming on in my apartment, though, and the refrigerator isn't going to magically fill itself with food. I can't be struggling here when I should be closer to my family in Farcliff.

Taking my father's place at Westhill is my only choice— even if I won't admit that to my parents.

∽

# ALSO BY LILIAN MONROE

For all books, visit:

www.lilianmonroe.com

### Brother's Best Friend Romance

Shouldn't Want You

Can't Have You

Don't Need You

Won't Miss You

### Military Romance

His Vow

His Oath

His Word

The Complete Protector Series

### Enemies to Lovers Romance

Hate at First Sight

Loathe at First Sight

Despise at First Sight

The Complete Love/Hate Series

### Secret Baby/Accidental Pregnancy Romance:

Knocked Up by the CEO

Knocked Up by the Single Dad

Knocked Up...Again!

Knocked Up by the Billionaire's Son

The Complete Unexpected Series


Yours for Christmas

Bad Prince

Heartless Prince

Cruel Prince

Broken Prince

Wicked Prince

Wrong Prince


**<u>Fake Engagement/ Fake Marriage Romance:</u>**

Engaged to Mr. Right

Engaged to Mr. Wrong

Engaged to Mr. Perfect

Mr Right: The Complete Fake Engagement Series


**<u>Mountain Man Romance:</u>**

Lie to Me

Swear to Me

Run to Me

The Complete Clarke Brothers Series


**<u>Extra-Steamy Rock Star Romance:</u>**

Garrett

Maddox

Carter

The Complete Rock Hard Series

<u>**Sexy Doctors:**</u>

Doctor O

Doctor D

Doctor L

The Complete Doctor's Orders Series

<u>**Time Travel Romance:**</u>

The Cause

<u>**A little something different:**</u>

Second Chance: A Rockstar Romance in North Korea

www.ingramcontent.com/pod-product-compliance
Lightning Source LLC
Chambersburg PA
CBHW010551170726
48285CB00011B/2855